"Who are you prote

"No one," she lied
What difference d

"It shouldn't matter,
vinced you loved me

Heather needed all her self-restraint to keep from blurting out the truth about her son's real father.

Dylan turned away and, as if in shock and functioning by rote, picked up the folder containing the boy's medical records.

"I'll take that." She attempted to snatch it from him, but he stepped beyond her reach, flipped the folder open and began to read. Heather was paralyzed with mixed emotions.

He glanced up from the doctor's records and gaped at her. "Chip is his nickname?"

Clasping her arms around her midriff in a futile attempt to stop trembling, she nodded.

"His legal name is Dylan Wade Taylor?" He stumbled to the bed and sank onto it as if his legs had given way.

She nodded again, numbly.

Awe filled his face, and she longed to touch the strong curve of his jaw, so like Chip's. "He's *my* son?"

ABOUT THE AUTHOR

Charlotte Douglas has worked as a college English instructor, an actress, journalist and even a church musician, but she enjoys most creating romantic mysteries packed with suspense. In *First-Class Father*, the follow-up companion to Susan Kearney's *Priority Male* in Harlequin Intrigue's RETURN TO SENDER series, she uses a fictional setting of her small town, an antique hunters' mecca on Florida's west coast, where she lives with her husband and two cairn terriers.

Books by Charlotte Douglas

HARLEQUIN INTRIGUE

380—DREAM MAKER
434—BEN'S WIFE

HARLEQUIN AMERICAN ROMANCE

591—IT'S ABOUT TIME
623—BRINGING UP BABY

First-Class Father
Charlotte Douglas

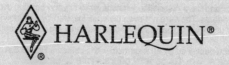

HARLEQUIN®

TORONTO • NEW YORK • LONDON
AMSTERDAM • PARIS • SYDNEY • HAMBURG
STOCKHOLM • ATHENS • TOKYO • MILAN • MADRID
PRAGUE • WARSAW • BUDAPEST • AUCKLAND

ISBN 0-373-22482-6

FIRST-CLASS FATHER

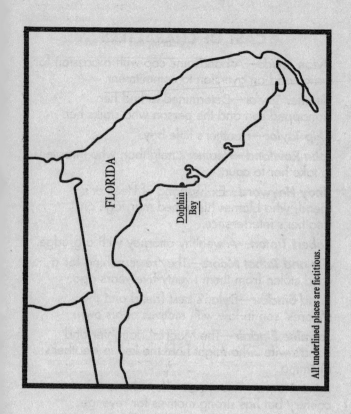

FLORIDA

Dolphin
Bay

All underlined places are fictitious.

CAST OF CHARACTERS

Dylan Wade—A handsome cop with a passion for justice and an aversion to commitment.

Heather Taylor—Determined to find her kidnapped son and the person who stalks her.

Chip Taylor—Heather's little boy.

John Rowland—Heather's neighbor, who threatens to take her to court.

Andy Hayward—Ex-husband of Heather's friend, who blames his ruined marriage on Heather's interference.

Robert Tipton—A wealthy attorney with a grudge.

Lily and Talbot Moore—They're searching for a child stolen from them twenty-five years ago.

Rand Sinclair—Dylan's best friend and the Moores' son-in-law with motives of his own.

Jasmine Sinclair—The Moores' daughter and Rand's wife, who might hold the key to Heather's dilemma.

Irene Moore—Talbot's ex-wife, who is out of the country but has strong motives for revenge.

Charles Wilcox—Irene's brother, in jail for kidnapping Lily, and for the attempted murders of Jasmine and Talbot.

T.J., Art and Blain—Sons of Talbot and Irene and heirs to Talbot's considerable fortune.

Prologue

Jacaranda trees in full bloom arched above the street in a lavender blue haze, blocking the glare of the Florida midday sun. A gulf breeze ruffled the lacy branches and rained delicate blossoms like ticker-tape confetti onto the lawns and pavement below.

Lily Moore relaxed against the luxurious back seat of her son-in-law's car and smiled. It was a fitting homecoming.

Beside her, her husband, Talbot, reached for her hand. She could see her happiness reflected in his eyes. Their European honeymoon had ended, but their life together was just beginning. They had a twenty-five-year separation to make up for.

The car turned onto the street that led to their home, and Talbot squeezed her hand. "Close your eyes. I have a surprise."

"You're going to love it, Mother." Her daughter, Jasmine, green eyes dancing with excitement, swiveled to face her over the front passenger seat. "No peeking."

Lily closed her eyes and issued a silent prayer of thanks for being reunited with her only child. She had missed all but the first three years of Jasmine's childhood and the rest of her growing up. Now, at twenty-eight, her daughter was a beautiful young woman who would soon make Lily a grandmother.

Eyes shut tight, she felt the car slow, turn and come to a stop. Talbot released her hand, and she heard his door open, the sound of his footsteps circling the car and the click of the door beside her.

"You can open your eyes now," he said.

She squinted in the brilliant sunlight and took his hand as she climbed from the car. Before her, the lawns of Moore House stretched back to the oaks and the three-story Victorian cottage nestled among the trees. Everything looked...different.

"Do you like it?" Talbot asked. "I had the tree service thin the oaks, and I hope you approve of the new color."

"Approve?" Emotion constricted her voice. "I love it."

Her heart swelled with affection for the man she'd loved for almost three decades. Now he had brought her home to Moore House, where he had lived for almost twenty-five years with his first wife, Irene, and he had changed the house as much as he'd changed Lily's life.

Gone was the somber brown exterior, replaced by a lovely rich cream. The oppressive oaks had been stripped of Spanish moss and pruned to allow sunlight to warm the building. Moore House, like Lily, had been liberated from its depressing past, and its future, like hers, looked bright and shining.

As if to make up for all she'd missed, providence had given Talbot and Jasmine back to her. She glanced at her husband, still robust and handsome despite his years. Fate had finally been kind to him, too. He and Irene had been freed of the bondage of their unhappy union, and their sons T.J. and Art had proved their loyalty and competence in helping Talbot run Sinclair and Moore Construction.

The only dark spot on Lily's contentment was Talbot's youngest son Blain, who blamed his father for his mother's unhappiness and had refused to speak to him since the divorce.

Lily shook off unpleasant thoughts. She wouldn't allow Blain's pouting to spoil her homecoming. Talbot would eventually mend that breach. As far as she was concerned, Talbot could hang the moon.

Beside her, Rand Sinclair, her son-in-law and Talbot's business partner, lowered the driver's window. "Do you want to walk to the house or ride?"

She inhaled the clear, crisp air of mid-April and of freedom. "We'll walk. Meet us at the house and stay for lunch."

The car pulled away, and Lily looped her arm through Talbot's. Together they sauntered up the circular drive.

"Don't expect any changes inside," Talbot said. "I'm leaving the interior for you to redecorate to your heart's content."

He knew her so well. Nothing would please her more than turning the bleak mansion into a home, *their* home.

They climbed the broad steps, crossed the wide porch and stepped into the dark, paneled foyer. Eugenia, the housekeeper Lily had hired before they left for Europe, stepped out of the kitchen at the far end of the hall. "Lunch will be ready in a half hour. Your mail is on the hall table. Several packages, too."

"More wedding presents, I'll bet." Jasmine entered from the back hall with Rand. "Why don't you open them while we wait for lunch?"

Rand gathered several packages and carried them toward the living room. Talbot followed with a large parcel under each arm.

Feeling like a child at Christmas, Lily read cards of congratulations and opened packages to find a Waterford vase, a Boehm nightingale, a sterling silver candlesnuffer and a linen tablecloth trimmed in Battenburg lace.

"This is addressed to Mother only." Jasmine picked up a box, wrapped in wrinkled brown paper and marked with an Orlando return address. "From Leslie Stratton. Who's that?"

Talbot shrugged. "She's not from your side of the family?"

Jasmine sat beside Lily and placed her arm around her. "You're looking at our side of the family. Open it, Mother, and solve the mystery."

Her curiosity fired, Lily peeled paper off the dress-box-size package and lifted the lid. An envelope lay atop the tissue. She removed the letter and read aloud.

"My sister sent your wedding announcement from the Dolphin Bay paper, so I know you're no longer at the mental hospital. My mother, Janet Stratton, was a nurse there until her retirement two years ago. She died last year, but before she passed on, she gave me the package you'd left with her for safekeeping."

Lily dropped the paper as if it had burned her fingers and raised her hands to her temples where an incipient headache lurked. "I don't remember Janet Stratton or giving anyone a package."

Jasmine hugged her. "Naturally, you don't remember everything. Charles Wilcox made certain you were overmedicated all those years so you wouldn't try to escape and threaten Irene's marriage to Daddy."

Lily frowned at the painful memories. Talbot never would have married Irene if Irene's brother Charles hadn't kidnapped Lily and imprisoned her in that hospital. She pushed the unhappy thoughts away. Charles was in the state penitentiary now, and Irene, accompanied by Blain, had moved to a villa in France.

Lily stared at the package with a sudden sense of foreboding. She didn't want to look back. She wanted only to go forward. She shoved the box toward Jasmine. "Maybe you should just throw this away."

"Are you sure?" her daughter asked.

"Lily," Talbot said gently, "whatever's in there was important enough to smuggle out, away from Charles and his employees. Opening it is *your* decision, but I'll toss it, if that's what you want."

She hesitated. Maybe the package held something good from all those years of misery, something positive to look back on, instead of merely wasted years. She drew it toward her again and folded back the first layer of tissue.

"Now I know how Pandora felt," she said with a nervous laugh.

"Don't worry." In the chair across from her, Rand, his long legs stretched out before him, flashed a reassuring smile. "No matter what it is, the past is over. You have family to love and protect you now."

She nodded. No wonder Jasmine loved him. Next to Talbot, Rand was the most considerate man she'd ever met. She picked up another envelope, addressed to Lily Ross, her maiden name, and yellowed with age. She withdrew the single sheet and began to read. Dizziness assaulted her after the first few words and she thrust the page at Jasmine.

Her brow furrowed with concern, Jasmine took the sheet and read aloud.

"Dear Lily,
Forgive me for not stopping them from taking your baby—"

"What?" Talbot bolted upright in his chair, and the color drained from his face. He stared at Lily in bewilderment. "What baby?"

Lily opened her mouth to speak, but words wouldn't come. Her hands fluttered on her lap as if someone else controlled them.

"Finish the letter, Jasmine." Talbot rose, moved to the sofa on the other side of Lily and drew her close.

Jasmine, her face blank with shock, continued.

"I would have helped you and your baby get away, but Mr. Wilcox threatened me and my family if I ever breathed a word to anyone. I'm doing what you asked me to, though, about keeping your baby's belongings. I'm packing them away so you can have them back one day. I hope you find your baby. Forgive me.

> Janet Stratton."

"A baby." Lily felt as if all the air had been sucked from her lungs. "How…?"

Talbot pulled her tighter. "The night you disappeared, we were together—"

"That brief time with you," she said, "was my last clear memory before Jasmine found me. But a baby? Even drugged, how could I give birth and not remember?"

"Your loss of memory isn't your fault," Jasmine reassured her, then prodded gently. "Let's see what's in the box."

With trembling fingers, Lily lifted the last layer of tissue paper. Beneath it lay two tiny white gowns embroidered with pale yellow flowers and French knots. On a card pinned to the garments was her clear but wobbly handwriting: "My baby, born February 18, 1973."

She faced Talbot, her cheeks wet with tears. "We have another child, and I don't even know if it's a boy or a girl."

Talbot took her in his arms, and she pressed her face against the broad expanse of his chest. "Don't worry, Lily, we'll find our child. I promise."

She nodded but said nothing.

Her reunion with her daughter and Talbot had taken twenty-five years. How long would it take to find her missing baby?

Chapter One

Six weeks later

Dylan Wade rolled over in bed and grabbed his gun.

A bumping sound at the back door had awakened him from a deep sleep. Someone was breaking into his house.

He eased out of bed, drew on a pair of jeans and crept on bare feet to the bedroom door. The intruder was either an idiot or a crackhead on a dangerous high. Who else would break into a house at nine o'clock on a sunny morning, particularly the one house on the street with a green-and-white Dolphin Bay police cruiser parked in the drive?

A surge of adrenaline banished his exhaustion from his night on patrol. Flattening himself against the wall beside the closed bedroom door, he waited, ready to spring when his unwanted visitor eventually reached his room. He wanted the element of surprise on his side, especially if the intruder had a weapon. Heavy draperies blocked the sun, darkening the bedroom. The burglar's eyes would take time to adjust, giving Dylan an advantage.

In the kitchen, the back door opened and banged against the wall. Footsteps pattered across the tile floor, up the hallway and toward the bedroom. Dylan cursed under his breath. The intruder must have cased the house earlier. He seemed to know exactly where he was going.

With a calm gained from years of experience, Dylan flipped the safety off his service automatic and waited. Out of the corner of his eye, he watched the knob of the bedroom door turn. The door flew open, and someone raced into the room, on a beeline toward the bed.

"Police! Place your hands on your head and turn around slowly."

The intruder halted and pivoted toward him with raised hands. "Dylan, thank God, you're home."

At the shock of the familiar female voice, he almost lowered his gun. It was *her* voice, the voice he caught himself listening for every time he answered his phone.

But it couldn't be her. She had refused to speak to him for the last two years.

He reached across the open doorway and flipped on the overhead light. His ears hadn't fooled him. Heather Taylor stood beside his bed. She hadn't changed. If anything, she'd grown more attractive. Her bright eyes still seemed to pierce his soul, her oval face with high cheekbones, delectable mouth and freckle-spattered nose still glowed with health, and her light-brown hair, cut short and bouncy and streaked golden by the sun, still made him yearn to run his fingers through it.

He even remembered the chambray dress she

wore, calling attention to her tall, willow-slimness with its high waist, long skirt and buttons all the way down the front. He'd once undone those buttons slowly, one after another....

"Dylan, please—" She dropped her hands to her sides and squinted in the sudden glare of the overhead light.

"I'll do the talking." He had to do something to cover his surprise, to keep his anger from exploding. Old feelings surged, threatening to drive away his anger until he yanked it back again. "Don't you know that breaking and entering is a crime?"

She lifted her right hand to display a shiny object. "I didn't break in. I used your key. But—"

"Why the back door?"

His jaw tightened with the effort to hold his temper. For two years, he'd longed to confront her, to ask the questions that kept him awake at night. Now that he had his chance, the unexpected sight of her chased the questions from his mind.

"Why didn't you just ring the front doorbell?" The clench of his jaw made speaking difficult.

She collapsed on the side of his bed as if her legs had given way and lifted her face. Tears filled her eyes, and panic, an emotion he'd never associated with the practical and efficient Heather, twisted her features. He hardened his heart and squelched the desire to take her in his arms. She'd walked out on him without a word, and now, obviously in some kind of trouble, she expected *him* to bail her out.

"I couldn't risk being seen. I need your help," she said, verifying his hunch. "Please—"

"You've got *some* nerve."

He flicked the safety on his gun, stomped across the room and shoved the automatic into its holster on the table beside the bed. A man as ticked off as he was shouldn't have a loaded gun in his hand. Besides, if he'd looked into those tear-drenched eyes another second, the feelings he'd tried to purge for the last two years would have made him do something he'd regret, like kissing her breathless.

"I don't want your help for me." Desperation elevated the pitch of her voice. "It's for my baby."

Her unexpected appearance had hit him like a sucker punch, but learning that she had a child, he felt he was going down for the count. He cleared his throat, not trusting his voice. "Baby?"

"My boy, Chip."

A baby. That certainly put a new twist on things. Unwelcome suspicions crystallized in his mind. "How old is he?"

"He just turned one." Her words tumbled out too fast, as if she'd rehearsed them.

A one-year-old baby. Dylan worked some mental arithmetic. The kid had been conceived only three months after Heather walked out of his life. Maybe the father had been the cause of her leaving.

"Please." She wrung her hands in her lap and choked back a sob. Her distress reproached his resentful heart. "He's been kidnapped. You have to help me find him."

And what would he get from helping her, except more heartache? "Why me? Shouldn't your husband be handling this?"

She looked dazed, ready to go into shock. "Husband?"

"The boy's father."

"There was a…car accident." She stumbled over the words. "He's been dead a long time."

He slammed the lid on his brief flare of sympathy and squelched a hundred personal questions he longed to ask. He had ached from missing her, had longed to talk to her again, but not like this. The sight of her had wrung his emotions and hung them out to dry. With the pleading look on that unforgettable face and the quiver of her soft lips, how could he maintain the cool detachment needed for dealing with a kidnapping? An abducted child was the kind of case every police officer dreaded. Too often the outcome was tragic. Shoving personal feelings aside, he let his training take over. "Tell me what happened."

Heather drew a shuddering breath. "This morning, I dropped Chip off at day care—"

"In St. Petersburg?"

She nodded.

"Why didn't you alert the St. Pete police instead of coming here?"

Her moss-green eyes, flecked with brown, were pools of misery. "He says he'll kill Chip if I go to the police."

"The kidnapper? You know him?"

She shook her head. "I never saw him before. When I took Chip out of his car seat, the man came up behind, grabbed me and forced us toward his car."

"He tried to take both of you?"

"I thought so at first." She raked her fingers through her hair in a characteristic gesture of impatience he'd once found endearing. "But I'm not sure. Look, can't I explain in the car? He already has a half hour's head start."

Heather was making a valiant attempt to hold herself together, but to Dylan's trained eye, she was only inches from hysteria. He knelt before her and grasped her gently by the shoulders. "It's doubtful we'll pick up his trail now. We should go back to your house and wait."

"Wait? You're crazy if you think I'll sit around doing nothing while some…some pervert has my baby!" Her composure shattered and sobs racked her.

He pulled her into his arms, trying to ignore how right she felt in his embrace again. He tamped down dangerous emotions. She had hurt him once. He wouldn't let her break his heart again. Steeling himself against her softness, he held her until her weeping eased, then released her, grasped her chin and tilted her face toward his. "If you want my help, you'll have to trust me, okay?"

She nodded, and the familiar fragrance from her hair, a subtle scent of orange blossoms, triggered memories, more yearning. He reached for a box of tissues on the bedside table and handed it to her. "It'll only take a minute for me to dress."

He grabbed socks and a shirt from his bureau and pulled them on hurriedly. After lacing on a pair of work boots, he slid his shield into the back pocket of his jeans and attached his holstered gun to his belt.

When he turned toward her, she had pushed to her feet, and a contradictory combination of panic and determination radiated from her in waves. Tender-

ness spilled through him at her courage, but he
shoved it aside. She loved another man and had come
to Dylan to save another man's child. Because Dylan
was a cop, he would try to help. Heather was just
another case. At least, that's what he kept telling
himself.

"Let's go." He lifted her by the elbow and guided
her toward the bedroom door.

"The back way," she insisted. "I can't chance the
kidnapper seeing me here. My car's parked on the
next block."

He followed her out the back door, locked it behind him and sprinted after her across Mrs. Riley's
backyard. If he had a choice, he'd be back in bed for
some much needed sleep, but he couldn't refuse any
mother whose child had been snatched.

Maybe once she reached home, he could calm her
down and convince her to call in the local cops. He'd
stay until the St. Pete police took over, then hotfoot
it for home before she ground his battered emotions
into raw hamburger again.

On the next street, Heather stopped beside the
sand-colored Taurus she'd bought the week before
she walked out of his life.

"I'll drive," he said.

She was in no condition to operate a vehicle. In
her state of mind, she'd done well to survive the
thirty-mile drive from St. Petersburg to his house.

She handed him the keys and climbed into the passenger seat. He eased behind the wheel. The empty
baby carrier and abandoned toys strewn across the
back seat reproached him. Caught up in his own sen-
timents, he had wasted valuable time. To have any

chance of getting the boy back, he had to move fast and remain objective.

But being objective around Heather was about as easy as keeping dry in a hot shower. He started the car and headed toward the interstate, the quickest route to Heather's St. Pete neighborhood. "Did you get a good look at the kidnapper?"

"I was too busy fighting to hold on to Chip." Her words were forced as she fought back tears.

"Close your eyes and make yourself remember," he suggested gently, more shaken by her tears than he wanted to admit. He zigzagged through going-to-work traffic as if headed to an emergency call.

She closed her eyes and inhaled a shuddering breath. "The man wasn't very tall. Baggy clothes. He wore dark glasses, and a fake beard and wig, both black."

"You're sure it was a man?"

Her eyes flew open in surprise. "No, I just assumed—"

"So it could have been someone you know, either male or female, in disguise?"

"No one I know would steal a little boy from his mother."

The terror in her voice destroyed his attempts at detachment. "What about someone from his father's family?"

The question must have stunned her, because she hesitated. "Chip's father was an orphan, bounced from one foster home to another."

Not once had she spoken her dead husband's name. Maybe talking about him was too painful. Dylan grimaced. *Hearing* about him was painful enough.

"And none of your relatives would try to take custody?"

"That's crazy. You know my mom and dad."

She was right. He'd met the Taylors. They weren't the type to steal a child. He tried a new angle. "Did you see the kidnapper's car?"

"It was white, two-door, but I don't know the make. New cars all look alike to me."

From the corner of his eye, he watched her cry silently, not bothering to wipe away tears that spilled down her smooth cheeks and splashed onto her dress. He knew from past cases that, in addition to fear for her boy, she was suffering major guilt. Heather's conscience had always kept her on the straight and narrow, and her irreproachable scruples had been one of a thousand virtues he'd admired in her. He'd never been able to reconcile that quality with the way she'd dumped him.

His anger flared briefly until the sight of more tears extinguished it. He could count on one hand the times he'd seen her upset enough to cry—and have fingers left over. He squeezed her shoulder compassionately. "Did anyone else see what happened?"

She shook her head, dug into her purse and extracted a tissue. "It's always chaos at the Children's Center in the mornings. Parents coming and going, children shouting and crying. I didn't want to wait in the long line at the entrance, so I parked down the block. Nobody seemed to notice when the man grabbed us. It all took place so fast."

"What happened after he grabbed you?"

"I tried to pull away, but he wouldn't let go. He was dragging us both toward the car, then he shoved me."

Dylan clenched his teeth, and cold fury spilled through him. As much as he'd studied the criminal mind, he would never understand how one human being could treat another with such cruelty. He itched to put the predator behind bars for the rest of his days.

"I fell," she said, "and hit my head on the sidewalk. The blow must have dazed me. When I looked up, the white car was pulling away." She blotted her tears and blew her nose.

Rage at the kidnapper and tenderness toward Heather filled him until he feared he'd detonate from pent-up emotion. He rolled his head on his shoulders and breathed deeply, fighting for calm. Merging the car into interstate traffic, he pressed the accelerator.

"Dylan?"

His heart wrenched at the sound of his name on her lips. That one soft word hammered him like the most agonizing scream for help.

"Will I get Chip back?"

He gripped the wheel until his knuckles whitened. He couldn't lie to her. The outlook wasn't good. If the kidnapper wasn't known to her and had simply snatched Chip at random, the boy was in deep jeopardy. If she'd gone to the police immediately, and they had put out an all-points bulletin, they *might* have nabbed the kidnapper and recovered the boy. But now—

"I don't know, Heather."

He glanced at her quickly before returning his attention to the traffic. Chalk white, she wore the numb expression of one who had confronted her worst fear—and was about to be destroyed by it. He was torn between wanting to reassure her and refusing to offer false hope.

"I'll do the best I can" was the optimum answer he could give her.

"I know," she said with quiet conviction. "That's why I came to you."

HEATHER LEANED BACK against the seat and hugged herself in a futile effort at warmth. In spite of the steamy June day, she hadn't stopped shivering since Chip was torn from her arms. Every time she closed her eyes, the memory of his tear-streaked face and his cries for Mommy stabbed her like shards of ice. Replaying the kidnapping was driving her insane and doing nothing to help find her baby, but she couldn't stop the repetitive pictures in her mind.

Turning to Dylan had been automatic. During the past two years, every time adversity struck, she had longed for his quiet strength to ease her through it.

Adversity? She suppressed a bitter laugh.

Who was she kidding? For the past two years, everything—good, bad or inconsequential—made her hunger for his presence. She had sworn she would never give in to the yearning.

Until today.

When Chip was snatched from her arms and her access to police help denied, she hadn't hesitated. Instinctively, she had driven straight to Dylan's, used the key she had intended many times to throw away and begged for his help.

If she hadn't been crazy with grief over Chip, no telling what she would have done, seeing Dylan standing there, tall and bare-chested with his jeans unfastened, his brown hair tousled from sleep and his coffee-colored eyes almost black with shock. She had longed to throw herself in his arms for the comfort of his embrace, the healing of his kiss.

Even in her tormented state, she'd known better. He wouldn't have welcomed her. His anger at seeing her indicated as much. She had made the decision to end their relationship, and now she would have to live with that choice.

No, she never would have run to Dylan if Chip's life didn't depend on his help. If anyone could get her son back, Dylan Wade could.

To ease her mind from the unbearable horror of the present, she focused on the past when she had met Dylan five years ago at the university in Tampa, had initially noticed him the first night of class.

How could she not? Every woman in the room had been aflutter over the tall, athletic man in the back row who looked as if he belonged on a movie screen instead of in a classroom. He had seemed oblivious to their attention. Polite but aloof, he had kept his distance from all of them.

One rainy night in late October, the class ran overtime, and the dark campus and dimly lit parking lot were almost deserted when Heather hurried to her car. After a futile attempt to start the engine, she realized she'd forgotten earlier to turn off her headlights. Her battery was dead, the rain still poured, and the nearest phone was a dark, soggy quarter-mile across the now empty campus.

She stifled a scream when someone rapped on her window.

"You okay?" The good-looking man from the back row, rain sluicing over high cheekbones and spiking his thick lashes, stood beside the driver's door.

She rolled down her window a couple of inches. "Dead battery."

He flashed a compassionate grin that warmed her in spite of the cold night and her damp clothes. "I'll be right back."

Within minutes, he jump-started her car, then insisted on following her home to make certain the engine didn't quit on her. She invited him into her apartment to dry off.

"I don't usually ask in people I don't know." She was babbling and couldn't seem to stop. "But you're soaked to the skin, and it seemed the least—"

When he removed his sodden jacket, she spotted the gun in the waist of his jeans at the small of his back. He must have seen the panic in her eyes.

"Don't worry. I'm a cop."

She inched her way toward the phone with its pre-programmed 911 button and mentally kicked herself for bringing a stranger, however helpful, into her home.

"Sorry," she said breathlessly, "but that explanation's not very reassuring. It reminds me of 'the check's in the mail' or 'we're the government and we're here to help you.'"

Except a late payment or bureaucratic red tape couldn't inflict physical harm. She relaxed when his

Dolphin Bay Police Department ID confirmed his identity, then apologized for jumping to conclusions.

He settled at her kitchen table as comfortably as if he lived there, and she poured hot coffee and served tiramisu from her stash in the refrigerator. "Sorry, but I'm fresh out of doughnuts."

Evidently aware of the scare his gun had given her, he smiled at her feeble attempt at humor and took a bite of the rich dessert. He lifted his eyebrows in appreciation. "Great stuff. You make it yourself?"

At his gorgeous smile, she fell for him like a plane dropping in an air pocket. She'd never believed in love at first sight, but what else explained the all-over tingle, the flip-flop in her stomach, her sudden oxygen deprivation and the tremble in her hands?

She settled across the table and cradled her coffee mug to still her shaking fingers. "I wait tables at an Italian restaurant. Free tiramisu is one of the perks."

"Must be tough, working and going to school full-time."

Wariness clashed with her warm, fuzzy feelings. "How do you know I'm a full-time student?"

He shrugged. "I've seen you in the library, and you carry several different textbooks from the one we use in Professor Aldrich's class."

"Are you always so observant?" What she wanted to ask was whether he'd noticed her particularly or if he paid that much attention to everyone.

"Being observant is critical in police work."

His appealing, slow smile and the hot coffee chased away her hesitation, and in spite of his heart-stopping good looks and her turbulent reaction to him, she felt at ease, as if he were an old buddy she'd known forever. They talked until almost six in the morning. He wouldn't have left then, but his shift started at seven.

They became good friends long before they were lovers, having discovered they shared similar qualities, reflected in their career choices. She was working toward her degree in education, and he had already served three years on the police force. He taught her to appreciate the nuances of professional basketball, and she initiated him to the wackiness of British comedy.

A few months after they met, Dylan invited her to dinner. She'd visited his house in Dolphin Bay before, usually as one of his many friends invited for cookouts and to watch basketball on his big-screen television. That night, however, hers was the only car parked in the drive beside Dylan's 1920s bungalow.

In the small dining room, candles glowed on a table set for two and centered with fragrant flowers. She didn't remember the meal he served, but his heated look afterward when he led her to the sofa, took her in his arms and kissed her for the first time was etched in her mind forever.

Later, when she could finally draw breath, she had snuggled against his chest, warm and contented.

"If I'd known how good kissing you would be," he said, gliding his hands over her shoulders, then pulling her closer, "I wouldn't have waited so long."

Pleased by his admission, she lifted her head and gazed into his languorous brown eyes. "I had reconciled myself to being your buddy forever. When did you change your mind?"

With gentle fingers, he brushed her hair back from

her face, a simple, tender gesture that seemed suddenly erotic. "I've wanted to kiss you from the first day I saw you."

"Me, too, but I never guessed—"

"I was afraid." His brown eyes glowed like ebony in the soft light, his expression as serious as she'd ever seen it.

She sat upright in surprise. "Dylan Wade, I've never known you to be afraid of anything."

A haunted look filled his eyes. He pulled her against him and held her as if he feared she'd try to leave. "You're my best friend. I don't want anything to spoil that."

"What made you decide to risk it now?"

"They taught us at the police academy to banish our fears by facing them. I decided it was time to face this one."

"And is it banished?"

He cradled her face in his hands and lowered his lips toward hers with a teasing smile. "Not yet. I'd better face it awhile longer."

Over the next few years, their love had grown, never detracting from their friendship.

"We're almost there." Dylan's voice jerked her back to the present.

The horrible reality she had held at bay with her fondest memories returned, clawing at her like a rabid beast, and she choked back a strangled sob.

My baby!

They'd left the interstate and were driving through the North St. Petersburg neighborhood where she lived. Dylan turned onto her street and pulled into her driveway. The sight of Chip's swing on the front porch stabbed her with fresh pain and guilt.

"How could I have allowed someone to take my child? Why didn't I fight harder? I should have scratched his eyes out or—"

"Stop it!"

The harshness in his voice shocked her into silence. She'd never heard him use that tone before.

"You'll make yourself crazy with should-haves." He softened his voice, and the warm compassion she remembered lit his face as he turned off the engine and unfastened his seat belt.

She longed to fall into his arms, to feel the security of his embrace, but she'd given up the right to that reassurance two years ago. All she could ask now was his help.

"What should I do?" She didn't try to conceal the desperation in her voice.

"Go inside and wait in case the kidnapper tries to contact you."

Her heart beat as if trying to escape from her body. "You're not leaving?"

The chiseled planes of his face settled into severe lines. "I'm staying until I've convinced you to contact the police."

She sighed with relief. Her control, like a delicate sheet of crystal battered by a high wind, threatened to shatter any second. Dylan was the glue that held her together, however tenuously. She'd fall apart without him, and then she'd be no use to Chip at all.

On trembling legs, she climbed the front steps and, trying not to think of Chip's happy giggles when they'd left earlier, unlocked the front door.

"Wait." Dylan grabbed her arm and stopped her from stepping across the threshold.

"What?"

"Do you have a handkerchief?"

She fumbled in her purse for a fresh tissue and handed it to him. He knelt on the mat, reached inside to the floor of the front hall and picked up a white, unmarked envelope that had been thrust through the mail slot. With the tissue, he gripped the letter gingerly between his forefinger and thumb, nudged her ahead of him into the house and closed the door behind him.

Her unsteady legs threatened to collapse, and she sank onto the parson's bench near the door. She had already guessed the letter's origin, and she dreaded its message.

Dylan took a letter opener off the hall table, slit the envelope and removed and unfolded the single sheet, taking care to handle it by a corner.

"It's from the kidnapper." His professional composure slipped briefly to reveal a flash of stark anger.

"He knows where I live."

Dylan nodded grimly. "He could have been following you for days without your noticing. Or he could be someone you know."

"What does the note say?"

"He wants a ransom."

"Ransom?" The word erupted from her constricted throat in a hoarse whisper.

"For ten thousand dollars, you can have your son back."

Chapter Two

"I don't have ten thousand dollars."

Heather slumped against the back of the bench as if someone had removed her bones. Sobs shook her slender shoulders, but she made no sound.

Her collapse rattled Dylan to the core. In all the time he'd known her, she had never yielded to calamity. She had always been a pick-yourself-up-and-meet-it-head-on kind of girl. Challenges or adversity had only stiffened her backbone and hardened her resolve. The quivering woman on the bench was a stranger.

He gave himself a mental shake. Who knew how he would react if *his* child had been kidnapped?

He sank onto the seat beside her, pulled her into his arms and smoothed her hair. "Let me call the St. Pete PD. Maybe there's still time—"

"No!" She wrenched away and sprang to her feet. "He'll kill Chip."

"It could have been an empty threat—"

"I heard him. He meant what he said."

Dylan sighed, torn between duty and—he'd almost thought *love*. Maybe his feelings were an echo of what had been, like a photograph of a time long past. He shouldn't care for her, not after she'd walked out without a word, refused to answer his calls, returned his letters unopened. She had cut him out of her life as ruthlessly and completely as a surgeon excises a tumor.

He shook his head. "The kidnapper *wants* you to believe him. He may have no intention of harming your boy."

"May I see the note?" She held out her hand for the paper he still grasped between his thumb and index finger.

Reluctantly, he passed it to her.

She scanned the contents hurriedly and her anger blazed anew. "'Don't contact the police if you want to see your boy again.' He repeats the warning right here."

The intensity of her fury startled him, but her ferocity, like that of a lioness defending her cub, was better than her despair.

"The kidnapper may harm the boy whether you go to the police or not," he said gently. "With the cops looking for Chip, he'll have a better chance."

"Do you really believe that?" She fixed him with an unblinking stare, and he resisted the urge to squirm.

His mind worked frantically, reviewing what statistics he could dredge up about child abductions. The advisability of bringing in the police was a toss-up. He remembered cases where brilliant detective work or a wide-flung dragnet had returned children safely to their parents in a matter of hours. He re-

called just as many that had ended in disaster.
"You're his mother. It's your call."

A guilty expression flitted across her face before
determination replaced it. "No cops. Not yet."

He pushed to his feet and rammed his hands in the
back pockets of his jeans to keep from reaching for
her. Old habits died hard. And with her refusal to
bring in the local police, he'd have to fight those old
habits awhile longer.

A shudder jolted him. She obviously no longer
loved him, but how much would she hate him if *he*
was unable to rescue her child? "Do you intend to
pay the ransom?"

She was making a valiant attempt at composure.
With her chin jutted forward and her lips clamped in
a hard line, she nodded. "I can borrow from the
credit union. I don't have that much in savings."

"I'll make coffee," he said. "You call the credit
union."

Without waiting for her agreement, he strode to
the kitchen. Funny how familiar her house seemed,
as if he'd last visited there only yesterday instead of
more than two years ago. He remembered Heather
using her parents' graduation check for the down
payment. She'd been ecstatic.

He'd been horrified. The house had been adver-
tised as a handyman's special, which meant, essen-
tially, it was a wreck. But Heather hadn't taken long
to whip the place into shape. She'd generated the
energy of a nuclear power plant, teaching high school
history classes all day, then working late into the
night stripping wallpaper, painting woodwork and
sanding floors. The only times he had witnessed her

truly at rest were those too-few quiet moments when she stopped her frenzy of activity to nestle in his arms.

Those memories brought more pain than he was willing to admit, and he smothered them as he reached automatically into the freezer where Heather kept her coffee.

She followed him into the kitchen and opened a drawer beneath the wall phone. After extracting a directory, legal pad and pen, she placed them on the kitchen table beside the ransom note.

With the quiet efficiency of the Heather of his memory, she sat at the table, opened the phone book and began jotting notes on the pad. Sunlight streamed through lacy ferns hanging in the tall windows above the sink and kindled golden highlights in her hair.

Observing her in the peaceful kitchen with its pale cream cabinets, polished pine floors and the aroma of brewing coffee stabbed him with the magnitude of all he'd lost, not only Heather, but the home they could have made together. Forcing sentiment aside, he reached into the refrigerator for the milk he remembered she took in her coffee. On the door, fastened by colorful magnets, were three of her latest to-do lists. Her obsession with organization hadn't changed.

Lower, at toddler-height, were crayoned drawings, indistinguishable squiggly lines and sweeps of color displayed as proudly as the most venerated masterpieces. He recalled the toys in the car and the swing on the front porch and wanted to put a face to the little boy who used them. "Do you have a picture of Chip?"

Reaching for the phone, she suspended her hand in midair at his question. Her expression had shifted at his mention of her son. After a brief hesitation, she said, "There's a photo on the mantel in the living room."

While the coffee brewed, he went to the living room and took a framed eight-by-ten from above the fireplace. In the vivid color portrait, an appealing towheaded toddler with a heartbreaking smile clutched a large stuffed dog beneath a Christmas tree. Dylan could almost hear him laugh. He had his mother's eyes and sweet mouth. The strong jaw must have come from his father.

Something significant about the photo niggled at the back of his mind, but he couldn't capture it.

He checked the mantel and tabletops for pictures of the dad, but the only other photo in the room was one he remembered of the Taylors, taken on their thirtieth wedding anniversary. He glanced again at the picture he held. Chip was no longer an abstract, a faceless kid. He was a real person who swung on his front porch and ran his trucks across the kitchen floor while his mother fixed dinner.

Dylan replaced the color photograph on the mantel and reached deep inside for that emotionless objectivity that helped him do his job unfettered. He couldn't find it. Instead, even when he turned away, all he could see was a little boy with his mother's smile.

Anger boiled where detachment should have been. If Heather had loved Dylan as much as she claimed, how could she have turned to someone else so soon after leaving him?

Unless she'd been seeing Chip's father all along.
He stomped back to the kitchen.

Heather braced herself against the counter with the phone pressed to her ear. "You're sure?" Color drained from her face. "Thank you." She hung up the receiver, swayed and gripped the counter's edge.

"Two days," she murmured, looking ready to faint.

He rushed to her, eased her into a chair and thrust a mug of steaming coffee into her shaking hands.

"Drink," he ordered.

She gulped black coffee and grimaced, but her color returned. Satisfied her light-headedness had passed, he thrust milk and sugar toward her, filled his own cup and sat opposite her.

"What's this about two days?" he asked.

Her fingers, long and tapered with pale oval nails, tightened around the ceramic mug. If the cup had been porcelain, it would have shattered from the pressure. "Two days from now is the earliest the credit union can approve a loan, even with my financial statement on file."

"How much do you need?"

"Fifty-five hundred."

"What about a cash advance on your credit card?"

"I don't have one."

He should have known. She'd always been fiercely independent and amazingly frugal. The writers of *The Tightwad Gazette* had nothing on Heather. She could save circles around them. The only items he'd ever known her to buy on credit were her house and car. For anything else, if she didn't have cash, she did without.

His anger rekindled, this time at Chip's father. Hadn't the guy ever heard of life insurance? But raging at the dead would get him nowhere.

"What about your parents?" he said. "Can't you ask them? They could wire the money from Fort Lauderdale."

She shook her head. "I don't want to tell them unless I have no other choice. Dad's bad heart might not stand the strain."

"I have some money," he said, surprising himself with the suggestion. "You can borrow what you need from me."

Tears misted her eyes and she ducked her head over her cup. "Thank you."

He had the money, and more, and he needn't worry about her paying him back. Heather would work three jobs rather than remain in debt. It wasn't the money he was worried about, but the thought of a helpless little boy who might not be returned even if the ransom was paid and what losing him would do to Heather.

Dylan winced inwardly. No matter how she'd treated him, she didn't deserve this.

As if reading his mind, she lifted her head and met his gaze. "The money *is* what he wants, isn't it?"

He drew a deep breath, weighing his answer. "When it's the child they're after, for whatever reason—"

Her breath hissed through her teeth, and her face turned pale again.

Damn fool, he told himself, *watch what you're saying. Her imagination is torturing her enough without you provoking it.*

"When it's the child they're after," he began again, "they don't send ransom notes. The fact that Chip was taken, apparently at random, and that the ransom demand is small, probably means someone's desperate for money and kidnapped Chip as a means to an end."

"So if I pay the money, I'll get him back?" Her eyes pleaded with him to reassure her.

Please, God, make it so, he prayed, and settled for an ambiguous encouragement. "This time tomorrow, this nightmare will be over."

She flashed a wavering smile. "We'd better head for the credit union. I have a withdrawal to make."

She stood and smoothed her dress over her thighs, and he noted the trembling in her hands. Her bravery rebuked him. In his anger and pain at her desertion, he had wanted her to suffer as he had, but never in his wildest, hottest rage would he have wished this agony on her.

A cold fist of apprehension gripped him. Her present suffering was nothing compared to what it would be if she didn't get her baby back.

HEATHER SCANNED HOUSES as Dylan drove past, searching for a white car in the driveways and any sign of a little boy with white-blond hair and hazel eyes. The cashier's check for forty-five hundred dollars was tucked in the purse on her lap. Later, Dylan would take it to his bank, withdraw the balance needed and ask for ten thousand dollars in twenty-dollar bills, just as the ransom note demanded. The note instructed her to deliver the money, alone, to an abandoned packing house in a citrus grove north of

Dolphin Bay at nine o'clock that night. The kidnapper promised to exchange Chip for the cash.

She glanced at her watch before returning her attention to the middle-class homes with neatly trimmed yards. Ten hours to go. She bit her lip to force back tears. Ten hours was an eternity for a little boy, crying for his mother. And for his mother, as well.

Dylan had suggested a sweep of the neighborhoods surrounding the day care center on the chance the kidnapper lived close by. At least, that's what he'd said. She suspected he had invented the search to give her something to do to prevent her falling to pieces until time to deliver the ransom.

A glance revealed the set of his square jaw, where a small ticking muscle divulged his tension. Only two things had ever disturbed Dylan's easygoing manner—flagrant lawbreakers and people who hurt others. Yet even when provoked by criminals or cruelty, Dylan never lost his cool. She had witnessed him, calm and professional, wading into a slugfest between two combatants and bringing order out of chaos without so much as raising his voice.

Sitting beside her now, his knuckles white on the steering wheel, muscles taut like a wildcat ready to pounce, he was angrier than she'd ever seen him. But was she or the kidnapper the source of his outrage?

And if he was provoked at her now, how furious would he be if he discovered how she'd lied to him? She clutched the shoulder harness until it bit into her skin. As hard as she'd tried, she couldn't help her attraction to him, but she couldn't change the way things were between them. If he helped rescue Chip, she would disappear from his life again, before he caught on to her deception. All that mattered now was her son.

"What did you tell the school?" An echo of his anger, like the rumble of distant thunder, underlaid Dylan's deep voice.

Worry for Chip had forced any thought of work from her mind until a few minutes ago, when she'd asked Dylan to stop at a pay phone for her to make a call to the high school office.

"I didn't tell them anything, except that I was taking some personal time. Today's the last day before vacation, and I've turned in my grades. My textbooks are inventoried and my classroom's in order...."

She was babbling, but she couldn't help it. If she didn't keep talking, she'd cry, and she couldn't help Chip if she was bawling her head off.

She sensed Dylan's tension ease, and he reached for her hand. She loosened her death grip on the shoulder harness and slipped her fingers into his. The warm pressure of his callused palm was like a lifeline. She could get through this, she promised herself, she'd have her boy back, as long as she had Dylan and his quiet strength to hang on to.

"I don't think this search—" with her other hand, she made a sweeping gesture that took in houses on both sides of the street "—is doing any good. I can't tell one white car from another, and the kidnapper wouldn't take Chip out in the open where he could be spotted."

He eased the car to the curb, stopped and turned to face her. "What do you suggest?"

"We pick up the rest of the money and go directly

to the packing house. If the kidnapper's holding Chip there, I can make the trade sooner.''

"Bad idea.'' The understanding in his tone and eyes indicated he recognized her pain. "We don't want to upset his plan. The kidnapper is probably jumpier than water on a hot griddle. We don't want to spook him.''

"But—''

"We'll go back to Dolphin Bay and withdraw the money from my bank. Then I'll scout the packing house area alone. I don't want us stumbling around tonight in unfamiliar territory in the dark.''

"I'm going with you.''

"If the kidnapper is around and recognizes you, he could panic and run.'' Or worse, his expression told her. "You can wait at my house.''

"Dylan—'' Fear for her child clogged her throat. She swallowed hard. "Thank you.''

An unreadable expression flicked across his stolid features, and he released her hand. "I'm a cop. I'm just doing my job.''

He drove away from the curb, headed north, and she shivered from the coldness she'd seen in his face. Tonight, God willing, Chip would be back in her arms.

And she would never intrude on Dylan Wade's life again.

HEATHER TAYLOR HAD him tied in knots.

Dylan stuffed the department-issue navy-blue T-shirt into his jeans and yanked the zipper closed.

One minute he wanted to drag her into his arms and kiss her until he couldn't breathe. The next, he remembered her betrayal and wished he'd never laid eyes on her again. If it hadn't been for the missing boy, he'd have sent her packing this morning the minute she'd arrived.

If it hadn't been for the boy, she wouldn't have been here.

He tucked up the leg of his jeans, slid a small revolver into its ankle holster and jerked his pant leg down to cover it.

Blasted woman. It had taken two years, but he'd nearly purged her from his system. Until she showed up today and stirred up all his old feelings, both his love for her and his resentment at the way she'd left him. She'd tied him in knots, all right, then torn him apart, until he couldn't tell love from hate or anger from desire.

He holstered his gun at the back of his waist and shoved an extra clip of ammo into one pocket. The other pocket held his cell phone.

"Concentrate on what you're doing," he muttered aloud, "or you'll cause a royal screwup and jeopardize that little boy."

He hefted his nineteen-inch Maglite, useful for both illumination and as a weapon, checked its batteries and looked at the clock.

It was time.

In his living room, Heather lay asleep on the sofa. She had refused to eat, and when he'd returned from casing the packing house where they were to make the exchange of cash for Chip, he'd found her pacing like a caged animal. He'd convinced her to take a sedative, prescribed for him when his partner had been wounded, and she had finally dropped off to sleep.

The rest of the day, drawn like the proverbial moth to a flame, he'd spent too much time sitting across from her, studying the sleeping face he remembered so well and trying to puzzle out what had happened between them that made it all go bad.

He had grabbed an hour's nap. He should have slept longer, but every time he closed his eyes, he longed for the sight of her again.

He leaned over, grasped her shoulder and shook her gently. "Heather, it's time."

Long, thick lashes fluttered against sleep-pink cheeks, and she opened her eyes and smiled in the slow, dreamy way he remembered from years past when she had lifted her face to his kiss. Desire flooded him until her expression crumpled, as if she'd suddenly remembered where she was and why.

Cold determination replaced his longing. He resumed their running argument. "It's not too late to call the police. They could surround the packing house and grab the kidnapper as soon as you've made the switch."

If the boy was there. He didn't have the heart to state the possibility that the kidnapper didn't intend to return her child. Her emotions were ragged enough already.

"If he were my son," he said, "I'd want the bastard caught."

Her eyes widened with a reaction he couldn't name. "No police."

He grimaced and acknowledged her decision with

a nod. Moving a mountain with a spoon would be easier than changing her mind.

She pushed her fingers through her hair and picked up her purse and the small satchel that held ten thousand dollars in consecutively numbered bills. If he didn't stop the kidnapper tonight, the ransom would provide a trail of numbered twenties to lead police to him.

"The plan," he said with more grimness than he'd intended. "Let's hear it."

"Can't we just go? We've been over it a dozen times."

"You're dealing with a criminal, not the PTA. You can't afford a mistake."

She nodded with uncharacteristic meekness, and when her chin trembled before she clenched her jaw, he could have kicked himself for his bluntness.

"I'm to drive north on Highway 19," she said, "to the entrance to the grove. You'll follow in your Jeep. I'm not to look back or give any indication that I know someone's behind me."

"So far, so good."

She took a deep breath. "When I come in sight of the packing house, I'm to park my car on the edge of the grove, in the clearing at the front of the building. You'll park closer to the highway and follow on foot."

"And what's most important?"

"I'm not to give anyone the money until they hand me Chip. Once I have him, I'm to run to my car and get out fast."

Her veneer of bravery barely covered her terror, and he longed to crush her to him, to vow that neither she nor Chip would be harmed. But honesty kept him silent, and old resentments kept him at arm's length.

She pivoted and marched out the door.

Twenty minutes later, under cover of darkness, Dylan crept through the citrus grove toward the packing house. A light on the loading dock of the distant building guided him to his destination. His footsteps in the soft sand of the cultivated rows between the trees made no sound. When he reached the edge of the clearing, he hid behind a thick growth of Brazilian pepper and drew his gun.

The naked bulb on the loading dock cast a puddle of weak light on the wooden floor below, where a small child, tied around the waist to an upright support, played silently with a push toy.

Bait, he thought bitterly, *just like a goat hobbled to attract a bear.*

Instinct and experience warned him of a plan gone sour.

At the edge of the clearing, several yards to his right, Heather, satchel in hand, stepped out of her car and began a slow walk toward the building. The boy looked up from his play and saw her.

"Mommy, Mommy." He dropped his toy, held out his arms to her and began to cry.

Dylan riveted his attention to the far left of the boy, at the gaping maw where the packing house's large doors slid back, exposing an inky interior. One person or a dozen could be hiding there.

"It's okay, Chip. Mommy's come to take you home." Heather, halfway to the dock, lifted the satchel. "I have what the man wants."

Her voice rang above the child's whimpers, strong

and unwavering, as if she faced kidnappers in the dark every day. She was only a few feet from Chip now.

Inside the open doors in the darkness of the warehouse, a telltale glitter of light reflected off metal.

"Hit the dirt!" Dylan shouted. "He's got a gun."

His warning reverberated through the stillness, a fiery blossom erupted inside the packing house, and the crack of gunfire split the night.

Aiming at the spot where the shots originated, Dylan fired and raced toward the building.

Chapter Three

At Dylan's warning, Heather tossed the satchel, but she refused to follow his order to hit the ground. Instead, she darted past the open door, flung herself onto the loading dock and covered Chip with her body.

Bullets whined through the air and thudded into the wooden planks of the building. A lightbulb shattered, raining glass. Chip jerked at each report, and his screams drowned all other sounds.

"It's all right, baby. Mommy's here," she murmured, with her lips pressed against his tiny ear.

Hunched over him, her fingers clumsy with fear, she fumbled in frantic haste at the knot that tied him to the post. After an eternity, the restraint fell free and she scooped him up, lunged from the dock and scampered beneath it. With her pulse pounding in her ears and Chip whimpering in her arms, she realized the gunfire had finally ceased,

Fear gripped her throat like a vise, and she struggled to breathe. Was Dylan all right? Or had Chip's abductor won the exchange? Was he now coming for her and her son?

Running footsteps pounded the hard-packed dirt of the clearing, and she scooted deeper beneath the dock, fearful the armed kidnapper was searching for them. In the distance, an engine rumbled to life with a roar and a vehicle pulled away. From the opposite direction came the blare of an approaching siren. Blue lights flashed between the orange trees.

She hugged Chip tighter and smoothed his fine, silky hair, whispering reassurances she wished she believed.

A police cruiser sped into the clearing, fishtailed in the sand and stopped.

''That way,'' she heard Dylan yell, and the cruiser took off again, siren screaming.

Relief flooded her at the sound of Dylan's voice, too strong, too vibrant for a wounded man. He was unharmed, thank God, and he would protect them.

The cruiser's headlights had ruined her night vision, but she heard Dylan's surefooted approach. ''Stay put,'' he said, ''until I check inside.''

She heard him swing onto the dock above them and walk into the building. Gripping Chip closer, trying not to transmit her fear, she held her breath and prayed the kidnapper had not abandoned an accomplice to ambush Dylan in the dark. She had cut him out of her life two years ago, as completely as if he'd died. She'd do it again tonight, but she didn't want him dead. Life without him had held a special kind of misery, but at least she'd known he was alive. If Dylan was hurt or killed, she couldn't endure the pain. Or the guilt.

She hadn't heard his return and blinked in the unexpected glare of his flashlight.

"You can come out now," he said. "The building's clear."

She tried to hand Chip to Dylan so she could crawl out more easily, but the boy gripped her neck and wouldn't let go. With him clinging to her, she scrambled into the clearing and felt Dylan's hands beneath her elbows, lifting her to her feet. When he released her, her knees almost buckled from residual fear.

The flashlight's glare bathed her again. "Are either of you hurt?" Dylan asked.

Heather ran her hands over Chip, checking for injuries, but aside from the emotional trauma the child had suffered, she found no scrapes or injuries.

"We're both—" she drew a long, shuddering breath of relief "—okay."

Dylan draped his arm over her shoulder and guided her toward her car, lighting the way with his flashlight.

"Bad man," Chip whimpered against her neck.

"The bad man's gone now, and Mommy's taking you home," she assured her son, who still clung to her.

"Not yet." Dylan opened the back door and cleared toys from the seat. "You'll have to answer a few questions first. The crime scene unit and detectives are on their way."

She sank wearily onto the seat and cradled Chip against her until his whimpering stopped and his grip eased. She couldn't face the question uppermost in her mind—had the kidnapper meant to kill them?—so she asked another. "How did the cruiser get here so fast?"

Dylan leaned toward her. The car's interior light

illuminated the taut set of his jaw and the worried crease of his brow. "I asked Tom Mackey, who patrols this sector, to stay close. When the shooting started, I called the station on my cell phone and the dispatcher alerted Tom."

"Will he catch him?"

"The car was a late-model white two-door. It was too dark to catch the make or license number. Picking it out of Friday night traffic on the highway will be tough."

"Chip's safe. That's all that matters."

"Not to me."

She shuddered at the venom in his voice and wondered if it was directed at the kidnapper or at her. When she burst into his house this morning, his barely leashed anger had been like a third presence in the room. Only when he learned that Chip had been taken did his cool professionalism take over, shoving that fury aside. Now that Chip was safe in her arms, Dylan could give his anger full rein once more.

But she didn't have to hang around and take the brunt of his hostility. As soon as she'd answered the detective's questions, she and Chip were going home. She looked into Dylan's eyes, deep brown pools of molten anger tinged with pain, and a tremor shook her.

Leaving him again was going to be even harder than the first time.

DYLAN STRODE ACROSS the tamped earth in front of the packing house, illuminated now by the white-hot lights of the crime scene unit. Behind him, Detective

Sergeant Sid Bullock sat with Heather in the back seat of her car. He'd been there almost an hour, no doubt asking all the routine questions Dylan had already put to her earlier in the day—and experiencing the same frustration at her answers.

In the packing house, technicians from the crime scene unit scoured for fibers, empty shells, anything that might lead them to the perp's identity. On the loading dock near the open doors lay the satchel with its payload in twenties, exactly where Heather had flung it when she leaped onto the platform to shield her son.

His gut wrenched at the memory of her throwing herself across the child, both of them too close to the crossfire. He had lost her once. And he had no illusions. Tonight she would walk out of his life as completely as she had two years ago, now that he'd given her what she'd come for. But if she or the boy had been hit...

Sid Bullock, short and squat with a face like a bulldog, stood at Dylan's elbow, perspiring in spite of the coolness of the breeze. He jerked his thumb toward the satchel in the doorway. "You thinking what I'm thinking?"

Dylan narrowed his eyes, considered the unclaimed cash and nodded. "Did the kidnapper abandon the ransom because he panicked or because money wasn't his motive?"

"I reckon he meant to kill the woman and kid *after* the payoff, to leave no witnesses."

"Murder for a measly ten thousand bucks."

"Lots of people been whacked for less," Sid agreed. From the level tone of his voice, he could have been talking about the weather. "Ms. Taylor says you've known her awhile."

"About five years."

"She can't think of anyone who might have a grudge against her. Can you?"

Dylan quickly cleared the ironic scowl from his face. He had his own resentment, a mile wide and two deep, but his personal grudge was irrelevant to this investigation. "I haven't seen her in a couple of years. From the time before that, no one comes to mind."

Sid's sharp gaze skewered him. "She's pretty closemouthed about the kid's father. Did you know him?"

"No." Anger boiled in Dylan like an unwatched stew. "She says he's dead."

"She gave me his name. The kidnapper might be connected to him, so I'll check him out."

Dylan clamped his jaw to keep from asking who the father was. The investigation was Sid's, not his, and he had no need to know, except his own blazing curiosity. He glanced back to the car where Heather still sat with Chip. "Is she free to go?"

"Yeah. I may have more questions later, but not tonight."

Dylan trudged over to the Taurus. Heather was strapping a now sleeping Chip, his angelic face blotched from crying, into the child carrier.

An unexpected tenderness filled him as he observed the child, who had Heather's best features without her delicacy. This kid was all boy, from his sturdy body to the determined jut of his jaw, evident even as he slept. Dylan resisted a compulsion to reach out and ruffle the boy's silky hair, and he shoved aside images of a son of his own with dimples flashing, who toddled on chubby legs to greet his daddy. Home and family had no place in this policeman's future.

Heather straightened, tunneled her fingers through her hair, then dropped her hands to her side. "I owe you a huge debt of gratitude. If you hadn't been here…" She shuddered in the warm night air.

He quashed old feelings and kept his voice cool. "You don't owe me anything. I was just doing my job."

Her eyes widened as if he'd slapped her. What had she expected? To pick up where they'd left off, after she'd treated him like something scraped off her shoe?

Anger and attraction battled inside him. Yeah, she'd dumped him, but the time they'd spent together had been the best three years of his life. He couldn't just throw her, and the boy, on their own, not with a kidnapper who'd tried to kill them running loose, a dangerous assailant who knew where they lived.

She turned and reached for the handle of the driver's door, but not before he noticed the tears in her eyes. His conscience pricked him. Just because she'd ripped out his heart and stomped on it didn't mean *he* had to act like a jerk.

Before he could stop himself, he cupped her cheek. "I'm glad you have your son back safe and sound."

For a fleeting second, she leaned into his caress before tossing her head and flashing a smile that tore at his insides with its sweetness. "I knew I could count on you. Goodbye, Dylan."

He dropped his hand and leaned against the door. Caught up in old feelings, he had been distracted from what he'd come to tell her. "You can't go home."

A myriad of emotions scudded across her face. "Why?"

He had to convince her not to go home, but he didn't want to scare her to death. "We're not sure money was the motive for the kidnapping."

Beneath the glare from the technicians' bright lights, the blood ebbed from her face. "If he didn't want money, why did he ask me to bring it?"

"Maybe he wanted to harm you and used Chip as bait." His words were gentle, but the ugliness in their meaning was clear. He ached to hold her. Yes, she'd hurt him, but she didn't deserve the horror reflected in her eyes. "That's why you can't go home. Not tonight. Not until Sid finds out who's behind this."

Looking shell-shocked, she nodded. "I'll find a motel...."

"I'd take you to my house, but I go on duty in a few minutes—"

"I've caused you enough trouble—"

"So my dad's on his way. He'll ride with you to their house for the night."

She raked both hands through her hair again, and her eyes filled with panic. "I can't—"

"Mom is expecting you." Her apprehension puzzled him until he realized Heather probably feared his parents held a grudge for her treatment of their son. She had loved his parents, and they had been crazy about her.

His mom had never dropped so many hints about

marriage concerning any other woman. He'd never told his mother how much Heather's desertion had hurt him, but his mom was no dummy. She had guessed.

"There's a crib," he said, "in the guest room where my sisters' kids sleep when they visit. Even though Dad's retired from the force now, he can keep you and your son safe."

"Your parents won't want me to stay, not after..." Her mouth worked silently as she fumbled for words.

"If they carried grudges against all my old girl-friends, they'd dislike half the county." He smiled with satisfaction at his quick comeback. No need to let her think he'd been pining away, even if he hadn't enjoyed any woman's company since she'd left. "You and Chip will be safe. The kidnapper won't think to look for you there."

"Okay." Her shoulders drooped as if she'd lost a battle. "But just for tonight. I'm too tired to argue."

HEATHER TUCKED CHIP into the crib in the Wades' guest room. He closed his eyes and fell asleep immediately, in spite of his unfamiliar surroundings. Her baby's day had been a nightmare she didn't like to think about, even though he showed no outward signs of mistreatment. She smoothed his soft, flushed cheek with the back of her hand and pulled a light blanket over him for protection from the cool flow of the air-conditioning. God willing, he would suffer no permanent trauma, and he seemed to be recovering already.

As soon as they'd reached the Wades', even through his tiredness, he had giggled at Mame, their fat little terrier, who'd licked the salt tears from his face and dogged his every step.

Margaret and Frank, guessing that the boy probably hadn't eaten all day, had insisted on feeding him. While Chip had gobbled glazed carrots, mashed potatoes and hot dog cut in tiny pieces, and slipped an occasional bite to Mame, begging beneath the table, they had encouraged her to eat, too. But food wouldn't navigate past the knot in her throat. Even if it had, it wouldn't have remained long in her roiling stomach. She had escaped one sure catastrophe only to plunge headlong into the likelihood of another.

She turned from the crib and unbuttoned her chambray dress—it seemed like a lifetime instead of only this morning that she'd put it on—and hung it in the closet. After slipping into the nightgown Margaret had provided, she climbed into the wide bed and left the bedside table lamp burning in case Chip awakened in the night. He'd be able to see her and maybe wouldn't be so frightened to find himself in a strange place.

Tense and edgy after the terrifying day, she hadn't expected to sleep, but she awoke at seven, alert and refreshed from a dreamless night. After a quick shower in the adjoining bathroom, she slipped into her dress once more and considered her options.

Dylan wanted her to stay with his parents until the kidnapper was caught, but she didn't dare remain under the shrewd and watchful eyes of Frank and Margaret. Especially Margaret. Without Heather's saying a word, those two would know her every secret within a couple of days, and she had one secret she had no intention of sharing. Not with anyone.

Going home might have its dangers, but she could minimize them. As much as she hated having to do it, she'd spend some of her savings to have a security system installed. School was out for the summer, and Chip wouldn't be returning to day care until fall. If she had to go out, she'd call a friend to accompany her.

Besides, she doubted the kidnapper would return. He knew the police were searching for him and would suspect they'd be watching her house. The clincher in her deliberations was the fact that, if she stayed at the Wades', she would undoubtedly continue to encounter Dylan.

Sounds from the kitchen and the aroma of coffee told her the Wades were also awake. In the crib, Chip breathed heavily, deep in sleep. Leaving the door ajar so she could hear if he called, she crept out of the room and headed toward the kitchen. She would thank the Wades for their hospitality, then awaken Chip and take him home.

When she walked into the sunlit kitchen, words of gratitude died on her lips. The only Wade in sight was Dylan, standing with his hips propped against the counter as he sipped a mug of coffee. His thick hair gleamed like polished maple in the sunlight streaming in the window behind him. His snug T-shirt and even snugger jeans emphasized his athletic build, but the impassive lines of his handsome face offered no clue to his thoughts.

Her pulse quickened and her insides turned soft and quivery. A man that good-looking should come with a warning label. She looked away to hide her reaction and reached for the coffeepot.

"I just came off duty. It's been a busy night."

She wheeled to face him. "Did they catch the kidnapper?"

He shook his head. "Mackey lost him in traffic. With dozens of access roads on the highway, he could have turned off anywhere."

Disappointment zipped through her, but her plans hadn't changed. She poured her coffee but didn't take a seat. She wouldn't be there long.

"We may pick up some leads when the forensics reports come in." Dylan rinsed his empty mug in the sink and dried his hands on a checkered towel. "They found a few fibers and spent cartridges that could point us in the right direction."

Her trembling hands sloshed coffee from the mug. The longer she stayed in the same room with him, the harder leaving would be. She eased by him and poured her coffee down the drain, but before she could turn to go, he grasped her by the shoulders and twisted her toward him.

"Heather."

The catch in his voice burned through her like a cauterizing iron. She resisted the urge to sway against him, the desire to feel his arms around her. She dropped her gaze, unable to meet the fierce intensity of his eyes.

He gripped her shoulders tighter. "There's something I have to know—"

"I don't have time to talk." She wrenched from his grasp and walked away, putting the kitchen table between them to protect her from him—and herself. "Chip and I are going home."

His startled expression indicated her announcement had driven his questions from his mind, questions she wouldn't answer, no matter how often he posed them.

He shook his head in disbelief. "That's not a good idea."

She placed her hands flat on the table to stop their shaking. "I can't hide forever, and Chip's been through enough already. He needs the security of familiar surroundings."

Dylan uttered an exclamation of disgust. "He needs security, all right, but—"

"I'll call to request an alarm system be installed today, as soon as I get home."

"And if it can't be installed today?"

"Chip and I will stay with a friend until it's ready."

His face darkened. "I know you can't see the last of me too soon—"

Her heart contorted in pain. For a man with great deductive abilities, he didn't have a clue.

"But I promise to keep away if you'll just stay with my folks a few more days. Going home's too risky right now."

"Maybe not. My guess is that the kidnapper's long gone."

"And if he isn't? He knows where you live, remember? He left the ransom note at your house."

If she listened much longer, Dylan would convince her to stay, but as unsafe as returning home might be, remaining with the Wades, even without Dylan around, was a risk she had to avoid.

"Thank you for everything, Dylan, and thank your folks for me, too."

She swiveled on her heel and left the kitchen, pleased that she'd managed to say goodbye without losing her composure. In the guest room, she scooped a sleeping Chip out of the crib, grabbed her purse and keys and headed for the door. She had to leave the house before Margaret and Frank awoke. Dylan had almost persuaded her to stay. She wasn't sure she could resist all three of them.

DYLAN GROUND HIS TEETH in frustration as he trailed two cars behind the sand-colored Taurus. Bone-headed stubborn, that's what Heather was. He'd remembered how competent and efficient she had been. He'd forgotten her ornery streak. That woman could make a mule look agreeable by comparison.

And what about him? Stupidity, not stubbornness, was his problem. If he had a lick of sense, he'd be home in bed, catching up on lost sleep, instead of tailing a woman who'd welcome another opportunity to tell him to get lost. His mama had raised him to have better sense, but no, here he was chasing after someone who'd rather risk her life than spend another minute in his presence.

But he couldn't ignore his instincts. That certain feeling in his gut had solved crimes and saved his bacon more times than he could count. And right now his instincts were screeching danger at the top of their lungs. He had no idea who was after Heather and her son, or why, but that unshakable, queasy feeling in his stomach suggested whoever it was wasn't through with them yet.

He followed at a distance when Heather turned off the interstate. He planned to take up surveillance outside her house. If she was lucky enough to have that security system installed today, he would alert the St. Pete police to keep an eye on her place. Maybe then he could leave her alone.

Who was he kidding? Only she knew the answers to too many of his questions, and this time, he intended to ask until she explained. If he had to live without her, at least he was entitled to know why.

Falling a block behind, he followed her through the quiet residential streets of North St. Petersburg. The roar of lawn mowers and leaf blowers shattered the morning silence as homeowners and lawn services hurried to complete their tasks before the day grew hotter. A peaceful, ordinary morning, the kind his would have been if Heather hadn't rocketed back into his life yesterday and blown his calm to hell.

He paused behind a U.S. Postal Service truck while the letter carrier crammed a mailbox with envelopes and magazines, then zipped around the vehicle in time to see Heather pull into her driveway several houses down the street.

He pulled quickly to the curb and killed the engine. Wishing he'd had time to grab something to eat, he slid down in the seat and watched as she lifted Chip from the back seat and carried him into the house.

Despite his irritation, he had to admit she was a good mother and that Chip was a lucky little kid. Together the pair disappeared into the house.

Dylan was twisting in his seat, settling down for a long wait, when Heather's front door flew open and Heather, with Chip clasped against her, raced out the door and up the street, in the direction of Dylan's Jeep Cherokee.

He sprang out of the car and ran to meet her. "What is it?"

Her expression of wide-eyed fear shifted briefly to stunned surprise when she recognized him.

"Somebody's in my house!"

Chapter Four

"Did the person inside hear you?" Dylan asked.

"I don't think so." The composure in Heather's voice contradicted the panic in her eyes. "Drawers slamming in the living room alerted me. The noise didn't stop when I turned and ran."

Dylan's outward calm hid his blistering rage at the trespasser who had terrorized Heather and her son. He hustled them into his Jeep, locked both doors and yanked his phone from his pocket.

The 911 operator answered instantly.

"We have an intruder—" He gave Heather's address. "We don't know if he's armed."

"Are you in the house?" The operator's voice was calm, soothing.

"Everyone's out. I'm on the street, calling from my cell phone."

"Stay on the line, please. There's a patrol car in your area. Help will be there soon."

"I'm Dylan Wade, a Dolphin Bay police officer," he explained, "and the intruder may be a kidnapper we're after. No sirens to scare him off, okay?"

"I'll relay your request to the officer."

He itched to draw his gun and barge into the house, but concern for Heather and Chip prevented such recklessness. If he stormed inside, they would be left alone, unprotected, and the man could flee out the opposite door and come after them.

Dylan looked back at his Jeep. Heather sat in the passenger seat with Chip on her lap. Although alarm had drawn the muscles of her face tight, she was smiling and playing pat-a-cake with the boy. Chip bounced and giggled, apparently unaware of the danger or his mother's anxiety.

"The officer is entering your street now," the operator announced.

"I see him. He's pulling up to the curb behind us."

"I'll turn you over to him."

The thickset black officer strode toward Dylan. "What's going on?"

Dylan flashed his shield and introduced himself. "When Ms. Taylor came home a few minutes ago, she heard someone in the house. Whoever's there broke in. I don't know if he has a weapon."

"I've called for backup," the officer—Parker, according to his name badge—said.

"Go in at the rear," Dylan said. "I'll cover the front. The intruder might be the man who kidnapped Ms. Taylor's son yesterday. Dolphin Bay has an APB out on him. If it's him, he's armed."

Parker nodded and drew his gun. Loping along the side yard in a crouch that kept him below window level, he headed for the back of the house.

Dylan knocked on the Jeep window, and Heather lowered the glass.

"Hi!" Chip said, with a megawatt smile that would melt glaciers.

Dylan's heart skipped and his stomach flip-flopped at the unexpected rush of desire to pick up the boy and cuddle him. He hadn't experienced such tenderness since his encounter at age six with a golden Labrador puppy he'd received for Christmas. The expression on Chip's face radiated the same hero worship Bear had given him until the day the old Lab died.

Dylan cleared his throat. "Hi, big fella. You and your mom wait here, okay?"

"Ho-kay," the boy echoed, "wait here."

"Lean on the horn if you need me," Dylan told Heather.

She held the boy close and nodded. "Dylan?"

"Yeah?"

"Be careful."

He sprinted toward the house and pulled out his gun. Waiting at the front door, he listened for indications of movement inside, but Heather's warning repeated in his mind, distracting him. Punchy from lack of sleep, he must be imagining things. For a moment, she'd sounded as if she cared what happened to him.

But she didn't. More likely, he told himself cynically, her concern came from realizing he was the only line of defense between her and the trespasser in her house.

Tensing at the thud of footsteps in the front hall, audible through the half-open door, he raised his weapon. A second later, Officer Parker stepped out and Dylan holstered his gun.

"He took off down the alley," the officer said. "I saw a white Mercedes speeding away when I reached the back door. He'd definitely been inside, though. The place is tossed. The homeowner will have to determine if anything's missing."

Dylan swore softly. "He's getting away."

"Relax, man. As soon as I confirmed the house was clear, I put out a BOLO to all units for the Mercedes. With luck, we'll pick him up."

Dylan nodded. The be-on-the-lookout-order would take care of the culprit for now. Meanwhile...

"Can you check the house for prints?" Dylan asked. "We need an ID on this creep."

"Crime scene unit's on the way. Bring the lady and her boy inside. I have some questions for my report."

Parker entered the house, and Dylan returned to his car. Heather was waiting with the window down.

"Did they catch him?"

Dylan shook his head. "He escaped in a white Mercedes that was parked in the alley."

Heather turned away, her lower lip trembling. He had always admired her strength, her ability to endure hardships and pressures that pushed lesser beings over the edge. Her incredible spunk had been only one of the reasons he had loved her. But the tremor in her lip reminded him that even a rock could withstand only so many blows before cracking.

Glad the car door stood between them, he resisted the overwhelming impulse to tug them both into his arms.

He opened the door. "You'd better go inside. Officer Parker has some questions, and he wants you to check if anything's missing.''

''Dyl.'' Chip grinned and stretched out his chubby arms. ''Carry me.''

Dylan lifted the boy. Tiny arms encircled his neck, a downy cheek pressed against his jaw, rough with beard, and the pleasant but unfamiliar fragrance of powder and essence of baby filled his nostrils.

His heart warmed until he spotted the cold shock on Heather's face. She had climbed out of the Jeep and stood, wide-eyed and white-faced, watching him with her son. If Dylan had been the kidnapper, she couldn't have looked more panicked. Obviously, she didn't want him around her kid.

With a sigh, he turned toward the house, still carrying Chip. The St. Petersburg police were on the case now. He could turn over responsibility for Heather and the boy's safety and exit her life.

He'd take off, as soon as he was certain they were protected. From the look she'd just given him, nothing would please her more.

HEATHER CURLED IN an armchair, sipped a cup of lemon tea and tried to decide what to do next.

The crime scene unit, Officer Parker and Detective Cramer had left a few minutes ago, after hours of brushing for prints, vacuuming for fibers and asking endless questions. Chip was napping in his bedroom, the one area of the house either ignored or overlooked by the intruder.

Her survey of the living room revealed desk drawers overturned on the floor and bookcases stripped, the volumes scattered with covers spread like the wings of wounded birds. In her bedroom, especially the corner she used as her office, the disorder was worse. Every folder had been yanked from her file cabinet and emptied into a pile on the floor, clothes had been tossed from the bureau and her closet cleared.

Had the intruder known her hatred of clutter and scattered her belongings for spite, or had he been searching for something? Her mind spun like tires in sand, and answers eluded her. Like Chip's kidnapping, the break-in made no sense.

Just thinking of the mess made her itch to put her house back in order, but she didn't want to awaken Chip, or Dylan, who had sprawled on her sofa during the last of Parker's questions and fallen asleep. The crime scene unit had worked quietly around him.

Conscience pricked her. Because of her, Dylan had gone without rest for the last twenty-four hours. Letting him catch a few winks so he wouldn't doze at the wheel on his way home was the least she could do.

She bit back a sarcastic chuckle. Who was she kidding? Knowing his presence was only temporary, she cherished every moment she could have him near her. Soon he would walk out her door, creating a hole in her heart as massive as before.

With a tormented sigh, she set aside her cup and saucer. Whoever had said "better to have loved and lost than never to have loved at all" must have been a masochist. She felt like her home looked, turned upside down and inside out. Maybe once she cleaned up the mess around her, her heart would right itself, too.

Another glance at Dylan shattered that hope.

Inflicting herself with the sweet agony of cataloging his features while he slept, she etched details in her mind to remember once he was gone. Thick chestnut hair cut short to departmental standards; a high forehead above dark, expressive eyebrows; long, thick lashes most women would envy; a well-shaped nose, unbroken despite his love of wild and rugged pickup games of basketball on his driveway; lips that had driven her wild...

Sometime later she awoke with a start to find Dylan watching her from across the room.

"What time is it?" She blushed, remembering her thoughts before falling asleep.

"Almost noon."

She started to rise. "I'd better check on Chip—"

"I just did. The little guy's sound asleep. Yesterday must have worn him out."

Thrusting away the unsettling memory of Dylan with Chip in his arms, she stood, took her cup and saucer, and headed for the kitchen. "This place is a wreck. I'd better get busy."

Dylan shoved to his feet. "I'll help."

She felt torn, hoping he'd stay and wanting the pain of his leaving behind her. "You don't have to—"

"I told Officer Parker I'd repair your back door." He followed her down the hall and stopped at the closet where she kept her tool kit. "Do you have any scraps of lumber?"

"There's plywood in the garage," she said, glad of the tranquillity in her voice. "If you're going to fix the door, the least I can do is make you lunch."

"Tuna sandwiches? Yours were always the best—"

As if embarrassed, he cut his words short, reached into the closet and yanked out the toolbox.

"If I can find the tuna." She forced a smile. "The pantry was ransacked, too."

For a few seconds they had fallen back into the easy pattern of their former relationship, and that brief revival made the ache of her loss all the more severe.

For the next hour, she shelved canned goods and restored pots and pans to their cupboards. She remembered how Dylan had always teased about the meticulous arrangement of her shelves and cabinets, unlike his own where he could rarely find what he needed without first organizing a search party.

With the outward appearance of domestic harmony, she puttered in the kitchen, while Dylan measured then cut a rectangle of plywood to fit the window the intruder had broken to unlock the door.

She was mixing ingredients for tuna salad when she felt the heat of Dylan's gaze on her neck and turned to find him staring at her.

He blinked, almost as if awakening from sleep. "The wood's ready, but I won't fasten it to the door until after Chip's awake."

Realizing she'd been holding her breath at the sight of him, standing in her kitchen as if he belonged there, she inhaled. "It's time he wakes up. I don't want his regular sleep schedule disrupted."

She hurried up the hall to Chip's room, aware of Dylan's gaze following her. Standing in bed and clutching the railing, Chip grinned when she entered the room.

"Out, Mommy. Want out *now.*"

A surge of love, so strong she almost gasped, swept over her. She had already lost Dylan. If she had lost her son...

She gathered Chip in her arms, lifted him from the bed and nuzzled the soft skin of his neck. "I love you, my big boy."

"Wuv you, Mommy." He planted a wet kiss on her cheek. "Go see Dyl?"

Her heart wrenched at the sound of Dylan's name on her son's lips. Loving and losing Dylan had inflicted her own private agony. She didn't want Chip to love and lose him, too. At the risk of appearing ungrateful, she'd ask Dylan to leave, right after lunch.

She carried Chip into the now empty kitchen, settled him in his high chair and gave him two small trucks to play with while she finished making sandwiches.

"Hi, Dyl!" Chip shouted with a happy laugh when Dylan, carrying the rectangle of plywood, entered the kitchen.

"Hello, fella."

Heather turned away, unable to bear Dylan's bright smile when he greeted her son.

"Lunch is almost ready," she said over her shoulder.

"This won't take a minute," Dylan said, "but you'd better plug your ears."

Using her battery-operated drill, he threaded screws through the plywood into the door frame. He finished just as she placed sandwiches and glasses of iced tea on the table.

After washing his hands at the sink, he sat at the table with the same easy manner she remembered from the night they'd met, a time that seemed hundreds of years ago.

"That plywood," he said, "will hold temporarily, but if you plan to keep a window in that door, you should buy a Medico dead bolt that opens only with a key."

"The security people can handle that when they install the new system." Her reply carried more sharpness than she'd intended, but his presence had her so muddled she couldn't think straight.

She stirred Chip's lunch of SpaghettiOs she'd heated in the microwave and fed him a spoonful. Dylan bit into his sandwich with obvious relish, but the turmoil in her mind and stomach ruined her appetite.

"Have you figured out if anything's missing?" he asked between bites.

She shook her head. "I don't keep money in the house, and I don't have any jewelry or collectibles."

A deep furrow formed in Dylan's tanned forehead. "Neither the TV nor VCR was taken. Did you have a computer?"

"I was saving for one. Guess I'll get a security system instead."

"Was the bathroom trashed?"

"That and Chip's room were the only places untouched. Maybe you frightened him away before he had time."

"If he'd been looking for drugs, he'd have gone to the bathroom medicine cabinet first," Dylan said.

"You think the intruder *wasn't* the kidnapper?"

"The break-in could have been coincidence. No car in the drive, no one at home. No alarm system and easy access. Maybe the opportunity was too much for the average burglar to resist."

"But why break in and not take anything?" she asked.

"Like you said, maybe we scared him off before he could grab the stuff he wanted."

Dylan's attitude, too casual and offhand, roused her suspicions. "You don't really believe that."

He shrugged and avoided her eyes. "If it *was* the kidnapper, once he realized you and Chip weren't here, why did he toss the place?"

"Maybe he was searching for the ransom money. Thank God Detective Sergeant Bullock offered to lock it in the station safe until we can return it to the bank and the credit union."

"Most folks would assume that much money would either be held by the police or returned to the bank."

"But it's possible he was looking for the ransom?" she insisted.

"Anything is possible." His intense expression added a multitude of meanings to his words.

Desire blindsided her with a fierceness that snatched her breath away, and she hid her reaction by feeding Chip another bite.

"Maybe," she suggested, when she could breathe again, "the kidnapper came looking for us or the money. When he didn't find what he wanted, he tore up the house as revenge.''

"This mess is the result of a hasty and frantic search, not anger. Aside from breaking the window, he did no damage.''

That disquieting thought remained with her while she finished feeding Chip and Dylan polished off another sandwich. If the kidnapper had been the same man who'd broken into her house, what had he been looking for? And why?

Money seemed the obvious answer, and, as she cleared the dishes and washed tomato sauce from Chip's face, she took comfort from her conclusion. Now that the kidnapper knew she didn't have the ransom money, he would leave them alone.

Out of lifelong habit, she made a mental list. First, she had to ask Dylan to leave while she still had the courage. Next, she would call the security company to schedule an installation. Then she'd tackle the chore of putting her house back together. She placed the last plate in the dishwasher and turned to wipe the table.

Dylan and Chip were gone.

Choking with panic, she rushed up the hall. In the living room, Dylan had placed Chip in his playpen and was collecting books off the floor.

At her sudden entry, Dylan lifted his head and grinned. "I know you have a system for shelving these. Dewey decimal or Library of Congress?''

"Nothing so elaborate.'' She sank into a chair and berated herself for fearing he had taken her son away. If she didn't calm down, she'd be seeing bogeymen under the bed next. "I separate fiction and nonfiction, arrange the fiction alphabetically by author, group the nonfiction by subject...."

She forced herself to her feet and tried to take the books from his hands. "No need for you to stay. I can do this."

His fingers brushed hers, infusing her with a tingling warmth that shot straight to her abdomen. His grip on the books tightened. "You have plenty to do. I'll shelve the books and watch Chip while you straighten your bedroom."

She broke the delicious contact by jerking her hands away and clasping them behind her back. Her mind churned, searching for a tactful way to make him leave. Her nerves and emotions were tattered. If he hung around much longer, she'd blurt out something she'd regret or, even worse, plunge into his arms and make a total idiot of herself.

The only way she'd get rid of him was to ask him, straight out, to go. "You have to work tonight, so you'd better leave. Please—"

"I'm staying," he said with unyielding stubbornness, "until Officer Parker says they've caught the driver of the Mercedes."

She opened her mouth to protest, but words failed her.

"So I might as well help," he added, with an infuriating grin.

Cursing herself for a coward, she chose flight over fight. She whirled around and scurried to her bedroom. If she couldn't make him go, avoiding him was the next best thing.

For the next hour, she soothed her jangled nerves by returning the scattered clothes to her closet and gained calm by neatly folding and methodically arranging her belongings in her bureau. If she couldn't organize the chaos of her emotions, at least she could wreak neatness on her bedroom.

The resulting tidiness brought no solace. Every time her pulse and breathing slowed, the sound of Dylan's low, rumbling voice and Chip's responding giggle blasted her peacefulness to smithereens.

Once she had returned her clothes to their accustomed place, still avoiding Dylan, she attacked her file folders and desk. She had almost finished reconstructing the contents of the top right drawer when a glaring absence struck her.

She sprinted through the hall to the living room, now straightened with books neatly arranged. Dylan sat in the birch rocker, reading *The Velveteen Rabbit* to Chip in his lap. Dylan glanced up when she paused in the doorway. Before he aligned his features into a neutral expression, she glimpsed a ghost of the tenderness with which he used to regard her. That fleeting view, a shadow of the passion they had once shared, almost made her forget what she'd come to tell him.

"I've discovered what's missing," she announced.

"What?" Dylan stood and placed the boy in his play pen.

"My address book."

"Oh."

His simple response told her nothing, but his clouded expression, like a storm gathering on the horizon, sent a shiver down her spine.

"Why would he take my address book?"

"Who knows?" Dylan's offhand answer suggested that he did.

"What use is my address book to anyone?"

"No use at all—" His inflection hung in midair, indicating something left unsaid.

She pushed her fingers through her hair with impatience, strode toward him and lifted her face toward his. "I'm a big girl now, Dylan Wade. In fact, I've been taking care of myself, and Chip, for a long time. I can handle unpleasantness. What I *can't* handle is being left in the dark. Why would someone want my address book?"

Dylan sighed, and his breath, scented with chocolate chip cookies from lunch, fanned her cheek. Unidentifiable emotions flitted across his face and deepened the brown in his eyes.

She retreated to remove herself from his tantalizing proximity. "Well?"

"You weren't home last night."

She rolled her eyes. "Tell me something I *don't* know."

A grimness settled on his features. "Since you weren't home, and then your address book was stolen, it's obvious someone wants to find out where you are."

The room seemed to tilt, and she staggered backward until her legs hit a chair. She slumped into it as if her bones had liquefied, and her worst fears surged back to life.

"The kidnapper," Dylan said, "whoever he is, isn't finished with you yet."

Chapter Five

Dylan swore under his breath. He should have made a fast break back to Dolphin Bay as soon as he awoke from his catnap. How could he leave now, knowing someone might be systematically searching for Heather and her child?

Instinct, the same inexplicable certainty that had goaded him to follow Heather home this morning, and logic convinced him of the danger inherent in the missing address book. The creep who broke in definitely hadn't fancied a mailing list for party invitations.

"We can't be sure the intruder *was* the kidnapper," Heather argued.

He opened his mouth to contradict her, noted the anxiety more prevalent than golden flecks in her eyes and tempered his response. "A burglar seldom drives a late-model Mercedes."

"He could have stolen it," she persisted, as if trying to convince herself.

"Stole a car, then didn't take anything from your house but an address book? You have to face facts," he urged gently. "He's looking for you. If he'd heard you unlocking the front door…"

Blood drained from her face, and she glanced toward Chip, playing contentedly with a push toy in his playpen. The sight of her son seemed to give her strength. She straightened in her chair, gripped the arms, squared her shoulders and raised her chin. At her show of courage, another of the reasons he had loved her, a strong sense of loss filled him.

"But he *didn't* hear me, and if he's searching for me somewhere else, that gives me time to have a security system installed." The soft lines of her face hardened as she added, "And to buy a gun for protection."

"You *hate* guns," he reminded her.

Her chin ratcheted up a notch. "A necessary evil for defending my child."

"What if Chip gets hold of it?"

"I'll buy one of those trigger-lock thingamajigs," she said with characteristic stubbornness, "and keep the gun out of his reach."

"You don't know the first thing about using a gun."

He recalled the times he'd volunteered to take her to the shooting range to train her in gun use and safety. Like many people unfamiliar with weapons, she had recoiled from the idea with wariness and distaste. Arming herself now was the worst thing she could do. A gun in her uninitiated hands, especially if she was spooked, could prove more harmful to her or Chip than any assailant.

He started to tell her so, but the ornery glint in her eye convinced him arguing was futile. She was a mother, protecting her child, and if necessary, she'd tromp barefoot over broken glass and burst through walls of fire to keep Chip safe.

He shoved his hands in his pockets to keep from trying to shake some sense into her. "This whole discussion is premature. I'll call Detective Sergeant Bullock. The forensics reports from last night might give us a lead on this guy's identity. If we can nail him, your problem's solved."

"Maybe the St. Pete police have picked him up by now," she suggested, but didn't sound hopeful.

Dylan suspected Officer Parker would have notified him if they'd collared the Mercedes' driver. Of one fact Dylan was certain. He wasn't leaving Heather and Chip alone in this house. He'd drag them back to the safety of Dolphin Bay if he had to kidnap them himself.

Heather pushed to her feet. She had changed her chambray dress for white shorts and a green, scoop-neck shirt before lunch. She wiped her palms along the fabric on her thighs, as if to hide their trembling. Her display of courage had been an act. She was obviously as concerned over their safety as he was.

"I'll start making calls to home security companies," she said.

He nodded. "I'll keep an eye on Chip while I contact Bullock on my cell phone."

Watching her leave the room, he identified another fact of which he was certain. He wouldn't let her walk out of his life again until she explained why she'd left him the first time.

WHEN HEATHER RETURNED to the living room a short while later, Chip was asleep in his playpen and

Dylan was pacing the Oriental rug in front of the sofa.

"Is something wrong?" she asked quietly, not wanting to awaken Chip.

Dylan scowled. "Not a thing, if you like dead ends."

Dead end.

The perfect description for her relationship with the handsome, irresistible and infuriating man who lit up her life like fireworks in the night sky. Two years ago, she'd hit one dead end when she cut off all contact with him. Yesterday, life had dragged her down an unexpected road and reunited them again. Now another dead end loomed at the end of this route as well.

"So you're leaving now," she said flatly, steeling herself for the desolation to come.

His scowl deepened. "Who said anything about leaving? I was talking about the investigation."

Heat seared her cheeks, and she bent over the playpen and brushed Chip's hair from his forehead so Dylan couldn't see her blush. He must never guess how much she wanted him to stay.

"Bullock gave me the forensic reports over the phone," he said.

Her composure recaptured, she stood and faced him. "What did they find?"

"Nothing, nada and zip, in that order."

"I thought criminals always left *something* at the scene of a crime, even if only a strand of hair."

His sharp laugh echoed in the room. "He left hair, all right. Several strands were caught on a nail in the packing house. All dark black, all from the same nylon wig.''

Heather sank into a chair. ''No fingerprints?''

''None. And none on the ransom note, either. He must have worn gloves.'' He ceased pacing and settled into the chair across from her.

Weariness mixed with frustration in his expression, and she longed to go to him and brush the hair from his forehead as she had Chip's. She clasped her hands tightly in her lap to avoid temptation. ''Didn't you tell me they found empty cartridge cases?''

He leaned against the back of the chair and nodded. ''The only thing that tells us is that he fired a nine-millimeter automatic. Once we find the gun, we can check barrel markings to prove it was the same one fired at you, but we're unlikely to uncover the weapon since we have no idea *who* we're looking for.''

Unexpressed anger appeared to boil inside him like a simmering volcano, and not for the first time she wondered how much of his irritation was caused by her sudden reappearance in his life. ''Maybe the police will find his car and pick him up.''

He shook his head. ''I spoke to Officer Parker. They've stopped every white Mercedes on the city streets. Every driver was an elderly retiree with an ironclad alibi for this morning.''

Disappointment laced with fear seeped through her. ''So he got away.''

''This time. He could be anywhere in the state by now.''

The menace in his voice made her shudder. ''You

don't think he'll come back? That he'll try to break in and take Chip again?''

He shrugged. "Returning this morning after last night's fiasco proves he's determined. A rational person might not persist, knowing the police are looking for him. But, since you can't think of a logical reason why someone wants to harm you or Chip, we can't assume he's rational."

"We're being stalked by a lunatic?"

His face reflected his reluctance to answer. "It's possible."

Conflicting emotions ripped her apart. She wanted Dylan gone. His presence taunted and tormented her with all she'd lost. And she wanted Chip safe. As long as Dylan remained in the house, the kidnapper, possibly a crazy man, had little chance of harming her son. But the longer Dylan stayed, the greater the potential for disaster of another kind.

Her head ached from internal wrangling. She latched onto the plan she'd devised a few minutes ago in the kitchen. "I scheduled installation of a security system."

"Good," Dylan said with overt relief. "When?"

"I checked with five different companies. Day after tomorrow was the soonest I could get."

He frowned. "You can't stay here until then. It isn't safe."

"I'll call Carol. You remember, she's in the history department at my school. She'll take us in until the system's ready."

His scowl darkened. "Is *she* listed in your address book?"

Her heart plummeted. Dylan and danger had muddled her mind. "Yes, she's in there."

"Am *I* listed in your address book?" he asked, his voice heavy with bitterness.

With flaming cheeks, she shook her head. She'd expunged him from every aspect of her life with the ruthlessness of desperation, a desire to avoid more pain. From the hurt and anger mirrored in his eyes, she realized he'd jumped to the wrong conclusion about his absence from her address book. As unbearable as his reaction was, she welcomed it, knowing she'd successfully steered him from the truth.

"If my name and address aren't there," he said, "the kidnapper won't look for you at my house. You and Chip are coming home with me."

DYLAN SWORE SILENTLY as Heather's blunt "No!" reverberated through the room. If he had harbored any doubts about her animosity toward him, the strength of her rejection sent them flying. She must despise him big-time to risk her own safety and her son's, rather than remain in his presence.

As if realizing the rudeness of her abrupt response, she flushed and avoided his gaze. "I mean, staying with you wouldn't be wise, since you're working night shift and—"

"I'm taking some overdue vacation, starting today," he said. "I cleared it with the chief when I called Detective Sergeant Bullock."

He had accumulated too many vacation days, he thought grimly. Since Heather had shut him out of her life, he had avoided time off. Leisure gave him unlimited opportunity to contemplate what he'd lost and why she'd left. He had postponed vacations and volunteered for extra duty and holidays, hoping activity would drive away his loneliness, ease his heartache and quench his anger.

But keeping busy hadn't worked, although the passage of time had dulled the gut-ripping sharpness of his bitterness and grief, until her appearance yesterday honed his emotions back to their original keen edge.

"Chip and I will check into a hotel." The certainty in her voice told him she'd worked everything out. Even if it wasn't written down, she'd probably compiled a list of all the details in her head. "The Bayfront Hilton has excellent security—"

The telephone rang in the kitchen. With the relieved expression of a reprieved prisoner, she dashed out of the room.

He sucked in air in hopes of loosening the tension her rejection had knotted in his muscles. She didn't want him around her or her son. He should feel grateful that her suggestion of staying at the Hilton let him off the hook, but all he felt was frustrated. He would follow her to the hotel, make certain she checked in, speak to the chief of security and head for home. Right after she'd disclosed why she walked out two years ago.

The sound of her raised voice in the kitchen cut through his planning. "Don't threaten me. We've been through all this before—"

He eased down the hall and leaned against the frame of the kitchen door. Heather, her cheeks flushed, the fingers of her left hand thrust through her hair, listened to the person on the other end of the line. Her eyes sparked green fire, and her soft mouth settled into a hard, grim line.

"So get a lawyer," she snapped into the receiver, "and we'll settle this in court."

His imagination stirred. Still stinging from her rebuff, he wondered if she had lied about the death of Chip's father. The little he'd heard of her side of the telephone conversation sounded like a custody battle.

She tapped her foot impatiently against the tile floor and wrapped the phone cord around her hand as if wishing she could strangle someone with it. "There's no point rehashing this, John. Have your lawyer contact me."

With a grimace of disgust, she slammed down the receiver, then sank into a chair at the table and cradled her head in her hands.

"I don't need this," she said with a groan. "Not today."

"Who's John?" he asked.

Her head snapped up with a jerk. "I thought you were in the other room."

"Who's John?" he repeated in a voice raw with hurt and anger.

Slouching in her chair, she met his gaze. "My next-door neighbor."

His convoluted thinking zoomed into overdrive. Was John next door Chip's father? And if so, why hadn't she admitted it?

Why should she tell you? an inner voice taunted. *You're nothing to her.*

"You're fighting with John over Chip." He failed to filter the bitterness from his voice.

"What?"

She was looking at him as if he'd lost his mind. Maybe he had. Jealousy, thick and cloying, threatened to choke him. This should have been *their* home, his and Heather's, and Chip should have been *their* son, not the child of a neighbor.

With superhuman effort, he reined in his disappointment and anger. "Sorry, it's none of my business."

Comprehension kindled in her eyes, and her expression softened. She giggled.

Spurred by her laughter, his outrage threatened to return. He hung on to his self-control, refusing to give her the satisfaction of thinking he cared.

"What's so funny?" he asked, with a calm he didn't feel.

"You think I want to take John to court over *Chip?*"

He nodded.

"But why…?" Her amusement vanished. Her posture stiffened, and her green eyes turned almost black. "You think *John* is Chip's father?"

"He's as good a guess as any. You never told me the man's name."

She clasped her hands tightly on the table, and dismay etched her face. "John is seventy-five years old."

Dylan forced his anger-tight shoulders to shrug. "So?"

"And Velma, his wife, never lets him out of her sight."

At her answers, he resisted the urge to squirm. His temper had landed him in a can of worms. "Why is he taking you to court?"

"John has an obsessive fear of hurricanes."

He shook his head, trying to clear his thoughts. Being around her was driving him crazy, because nothing she said made sense. "You lost me."

She pushed to her feet and pointed out the window over the sink. "Look there, just inside my fence."

He narrowed his eyes. All he could detect on her side of the backyard was well-mowed grass and an ancient live oak, surrounded by azaleas. "I give up. What am I supposed to be looking for?"

"The tree," she said, as if it explained everything.

He shoved his hands in his pockets to keep from tearing at his hair. This conversation resurrected memories of another of her traits he had almost forgotten. Making her listener draw his own conclusions might be a great teaching strategy with her history students, but her sparse explanations had often tested his patience.

Like now.

She expelled a deep breath, as if disappointed he hadn't figured out the answer on his own. "John is afraid my oak tree will topple onto his house if we have a hurricane. He wants me to cut it down, but I won't. That magnificent old oak is one of the reasons I bought this house."

He nodded, thankful he wasn't the blushing type. He had jumped to wild conclusions that had been way out of bounds. Then the ramifications of her words struck him. "How long has this argument been going on?"

"Since summer before last, when that Class Three hurricane missed us by only seventy-five miles."

He remembered the storm. It had crossed the coast

north of Dolphin Bay the month after Heather left him. He'd worked three straight days and nights of emergency duty, hoping all the while, in a perverse sort of way, that the storm would strike, blowing the rest of his world to kingdom come, finishing off what little remained after Heather's treachery. Mother Nature hadn't cooperated, forcing him to learn to live with his pain.

"What does John look like?" he demanded.

"I told you," she said with a hint of anger, "he's *not* Chip's father."

"Forget that," he snapped. "Just tell me how John would look in a black wig and beard."

"You don't think...?" Her face turned pale. "John *is* about the same size and build as the kidnapper."

"Did you give his name to Officer Parker?"

She shook her head. "John's harmless, except for his paranoia about that tree."

Back at the station, he had a stack of wanted photos six inches thick of men who had seemed harmless, shy and retiring loners until the day they snapped and committed horrible crimes. "The police should question John, just in case."

"I can't sic the police on my neighbor," she said hotly, "just because he hates my tree. We'd never be able to co-exist peacefully again."

"And if he's the man who tried to kill you and your son?"

Her hesitation was so slight, he almost didn't see it. "He drives a blue Cavalier, not a Mercedes," she said, as if that settled the matter.

"He could have borrowed or rented a car."

She glared at him, strode past him toward the hall, then turned in the doorway. "I'm going to pack. No need for you to stay. Chip and I can find the hotel without help."

Heather Taylor was, without doubt, the most stubborn woman he'd ever met. After trying to reason with her, his head ached as if he'd banged it on a wall. "I'm staying with you until you're safely checked in. Then I'll get out of your life again."

"Fine," she said flatly. "Suit yourself."

A few seconds later, her bedroom door clicked, closing him out as effectively as she had two years before.

Dragged down by fatigue, he returned to the living room and sagged into a chair to wait. Chip snoozed in his playpen, his features, so like his mother's but with a decidedly masculine stamp, peaceful in sleep. The boy triggered a thousand questions, but none Dylan could answer.

His gaze swept the familiar room, and happy memories filled him with fresh pain. When Heather came out of her bedroom, he'd demand answers. He wouldn't leave until she—

His attention fell on the eight-by-ten portrait of Chip on the mantel, the sturdy toddler laughing beneath a Christmas tree six months ago. The contradiction that had niggled in the back of his mind when he first saw the photo now slammed him in the heart with the force of a speeding bus.

When he could breathe again, he leaped to his feet, jerked the picture off the mantel and stomped down the hall toward Heather's bedroom with fire in his eyes.

Chapter Six

Heather's bedroom door crashed against the wall.

Certain the kidnapper had returned, she flinched and cried out. At the sight of Dylan on the threshold, molten fury in his eyes and Chip's picture clutched in his hand, she almost wished she was confronting her son's abductor instead.

"How old did you say Chip is?" The tightness in his jaw made his words almost unintelligible.

"A year old, this month," she lied, and edged toward the window, away from his rage.

"Try again." His lips twisted in a snarl. "My sister Megan's boy is six months old. Big for his age, his doctor says, and Lyle isn't *half* the size of Chip in this photo. So I'm asking you once more. How old is he?"

He spoke in a low, fierce tone, but his words bludgeoned her as if he'd shouted. The urge to flee goaded her, but he blocked her only exit.

"How old?" He ground out the words between gritted teeth.

If she could have run, she would have, but escape

was impossible. She had no choice but to answer. "Almost eighteen months."

He staggered as if she had struck him. "Eighteen months. Conceived three months before you dumped me? *That* explains your leaving."

You have it all wrong, she wanted to shout, but clamped her jaw against the words lodged in her throat. Better his misunderstanding than guessing the truth.

"Who was he?" Dylan's eyes blazed.

She struggled to remember the name she'd given Detective Sergeant Bullock, but her mind went blank.

"I have a right to know at least that much." He sounded more sad than angry now, and the rigor gripping his body had eased.

She blinked back tears. Her heart was breaking, clouding her mind with pain. She grappled wildly for a name, any name. Her glance fell on her four-poster bed.

"Ethan, Ethan Allen—bee."

Suspicion flared in his eyes, and she groaned inwardly. Why had she picked such a ridiculous name?

"And this Ethan Allen—bee," he said with sarcastic emphasis, "how did you meet him?"

Her thoughts tangled. She couldn't think, couldn't breathe. Her heart thrashed against her chest wall as if struggling to escape. She longed for unconsciousness to rescue her, but her traitorous mind refused to shut down.

Dylan advanced, and she pressed backward until her thighs struck the windowsill.

His anger turned quiet and more terrifying. "There was no Ethan Allenbee, was there?"

She shook her head, refusing to meet his eyes.

"Who are you protecting?"

"No one," she lied. "His father is *dead*. What difference does his name make to you?"

"It shouldn't matter, but I need to know. I was so convinced you loved me...."

She needed all her self-restraint to keep from blurting out the truth.

He turned away and, as if in shock and functioning by rote, began gathering files she'd abandoned on the floor when she discovered her address book missing. Her heart stopped when he picked up the folder containing Chip's medical records.

"I'll take that." She attempted to snatch it from him, but he stepped beyond her reach, flipped the folder open and began to read.

If she lived to be a thousand, she would never forget the fleeting expressions of joy and pain that crossed his face. He glanced up from the doctor's records and gaped at her.

"Chip is his nickname?"

Clasping her arms around her midriff in a futile attempt to stop trembling, she nodded.

"His legal name is Dylan Wade Taylor?" He stumbled to the bed and sank onto it as if his legs had given way.

Oh, God, after all I've suffered, and all for nothing, she cried silently.

She nodded again, numbly.

Awe filled his face, and she longed to touch the

strong curve of his jaw, so like Chip's. "He's *my* son?"

She surrendered to the inevitable. "You're listed as his father on his birth certificate."

His awe changed to outrage. "Why didn't you tell me? I had a *right* to know."

Her mind froze again. Her reasons for secrecy now were the same as they'd been two years ago, and just as strong. She couldn't think fast enough to make up an answer, and she refused to tell him the truth.

Before he could repeat his demand, Chip, awakened by Dylan's angry shout, wailed in the living room. Hardening her heart against the man she loved, she started toward the door.

"Where are you going?"

She paused in the doorway. "I'm going to *my* son. As for *your* rights, this is *my* house, he's *my* child, and the sooner you leave us alone, the better off we'll be."

FEELING AS IF HE'D BEEN poleaxed, Dylan sagged on the bed and watched her go. Two facts pummeled him until he could hardly breathe.

Chip was *his* son.

Heather *hadn't* loved someone else.

Her walking out on him, especially knowing she was carrying his child, made even less sense than before.

Maybe she *hadn't* loved him and had feared he would insist on marrying her if he'd known about her pregnancy. She obviously didn't want him around now. That fact pained him more than he wanted to admit.

But she couldn't just send him away. Chip was his son. The boy changed everything.

Righteous indignation propelled him into the living room. The sight of Chip, cradled in his mother's arms as his sobs ebbed, almost distracted him from his purpose. He searched for traces of himself in the boy's face before allowing his anger to pull him back on course.

"You're not going to a hotel."

She jerked up her head. "What?"

"I'm responsible for the safety of my child, and I'm not handing that duty over to some hotel dick."

She flushed and anger flashed in her eyes. "I'll make the decisions—"

"Don't argue." He softened his tone. "Chip's been through enough trauma without having to endure our squabbling."

Panic joined the fury in her eyes. "But—"

"If you don't want me around, I'll honor that, but I *will* make certain Chip, and his mother, are safe. I'm taking you both back to my parents' house."

Emotions flitted across her face, and he visualized thoughts churning behind her moss-green eyes. He feared she would refuse, until her shoulders drooped with defeat and she thrust Chip into his arms.

"I'll finish packing." She left the room.

With a mixture of uneasiness and relief, he shifted his son in his arms.

"Dyl!" Chip squealed happily, and patted Dylan's cheeks with his chubby hands.

Dylan clasped the boy close, amazed at the love blossoming in his heart until it threatened to explode. He was holding *his son* in his arms. Powerful feelings almost overwhelmed him, and he wondered why a love of such magnitude couldn't fill the chasm Heather's rejection had furrowed in his soul.

Suddenly a thought struck him, so horrifying it almost knocked him off his feet. In his years on the force, he had arrested dozens of dirtbags and slime-balls. Did someone else know that Chip was his son? Had one of them discovered Dylan was Chip's father and tried to harm Heather and the boy for revenge against the officer who'd locked him away?

If someone was striking at him through Chip and Heather, would they be safe, even at his parents?

He pushed those doubts away. If anyone else knew Chip's paternity, surely Dylan would have heard the rumors, too. And he hadn't had a clue.

Convinced Chip would be safest with his grand-parents, at least for now, he hugged his son. The police motto, To Protect and Serve, had just taken on a whole new dimension.

HEATHER CARRIED CHIP toward her car and started to open the back door.

"Leave it," Dylan ordered. "We'll take mine."

"I'll need my car—"

"Whoever's looking for you knows your car by now. You don't need to advertise where you are by parking your car at my parents'. As long as it's here at your house, maybe the kidnapper will believe you're here, too."

With a leaden heart, Heather removed Chip's car seat from the Taurus and turned toward Dylan's Jeep. She had given in to his unyielding refusal to allow her to take Chip to a hotel and agreed to return to his parents' house. If he kept his promise to leave her alone, she wouldn't have to face him again, wouldn't have to deal with his knowing the secret she'd guarded for the past two years.

She couldn't argue with his logic about her car, but she hadn't counted on the long ride back to Dolphin Bay, confined with him for thirty long, torturous minutes. To keep Chip safe, however, she would abandon her vehicle and stomach Dylan's anger awhile longer.

He moved with a quick, efficient grace, stowing their luggage, then Chip's car seat, in his Jeep. She locked the front entrance to her house, buckled Chip in his carrier and slid onto the seat next to Dylan. Sunglasses hid his eyes, but his death grip on the steering wheel and the tension in his body transmitted his fury without words.

After wrenching the car into gear, he turned around in her driveway and headed toward the interstate. Chip babbled contentedly in the back seat, oblivious to the strained atmosphere.

Heather leaned against the headrest, closed her eyes and pretended to sleep. Her ploy worked for the first ten minutes of the trip.

"Why didn't you tell me?" The question exploded from Dylan like a star going nova.

Confined in the car, she couldn't avoid answering, but she chose her words carefully. She wouldn't allow his anger to cancel the good she'd done them both.

"If I'd told you, you would have insisted on doing the *honorable* thing and marrying me." She colored her words with contempt. The effort scalded her like acid, but she couldn't let him guess the truth. If he knew how she really felt, she'd find herself neck-deep in the trap she'd worked long and hard to avoid.

His anger vanished, and the stiffness in his bearing yielded to sorrow. "You didn't want to marry me."

His statement required no answer. Even if it had, she would have lied and said she didn't, despite the fact that since the day they'd met, marriage to Dylan had loomed as the height of her happiness.

But he had never felt the same. They'd dated an entire year before he'd confessed his love for her, and even that assurance had had its limits.

The longer she had known him, the more aware she'd become of his aversion to commitment. One conversation in particular had burned into her memory. A day after their first lovemaking, Dylan had arrived at her house for dinner. From the gloom on his face, she'd feared at first that someone had died.

"Are you okay?" she'd asked.

"Sure." He roused himself from his blue funk long enough to kiss her as if he meant it.

Later, after a too-quiet dinner of chicken he'd grilled while she made salad, his contemplative mood deepened. They sat in the living room to watch the Magic game, and his preoccupation consumed him. When he didn't react to a referee's incorrect call, she withdrew from the circle of his arm and switched off the television.

"What's wrong?"

He inhaled, as if preparing for an ordeal. "I want to apologize for last night."

"Apologize?" His words shocked her into deeper uneasiness. "Why?"

Gazing at the dark TV screen, he avoided her eyes. "It shouldn't have happened."

"I thought you enjoyed making love as much as I did. I guess I was mistaken."

He turned to her with dark eyes blazing. "I *did* enjoy it. That's the whole point."

She shook her head and ran her fingers through her hair. "I'm not following you."

"I'm not cut out for commitment." Agony filled his voice. "Loving you like that—I don't want to spoil our friendship by sending you the wrong signals."

"Signals that you love me?" Anger battled with heartbreak within her.

"You know I love you," he said, with such intensity she couldn't doubt him.

"Then what's the problem?"

His sweet, sad smile tugged at her heart. "Have you ever watched a friend go through hell and felt powerless to help?"

"You mean like now?" She lifted her eyebrows in irony. "I can't help *you* if you won't tell me what's eating you."

Avoiding her gaze, he leaned forward with his elbows on his knees, hands clenched. "In the last month, three guys in the department have been hit with divorce papers. Today, it was Larry."

"Larry Shelton?" At a cookout at Dylan's a couple of months earlier, Larry, his wife, Joanie, and their adorable twin girls had presented a picture of the perfect family. Larry and Joanie were obviously in love and unashamedly proud of their daughters. "That doesn't seem possible."

"Believe it. Six weeks ago Larry almost bought the farm when he cornered a fleeing bank robber. Larry was wearing Kevlar, but if the perp had shot a few inches higher, the vest would have been useless."

"I don't understand. Joanie's leaving Larry because he almost got himself killed?"

"They've been married eight years. Every day, when Joanie kissed Larry goodbye, she didn't know if he'd walk in the door at the end of his shift or be carted to the morgue in a body bag. When she learned how close he'd come to dying in that bank robbery, she cracked."

Heather understood. She'd felt the same way many times, knowing Dylan was on duty, praying he'd make it through his shift unharmed. But she couldn't imagine not wanting to be there when the danger had passed and he came home.

In fact, she *wanted* to be there, had hoped he'd ask her to marry him. For the past year, although he'd said he loved her, had proved it with the fervor of his kisses and in a hundred more subtle ways, he had never once mentioned marriage.

Sadness darkened his eyes. "Joanie couldn't take it any longer. She said the stress was killing her and that her anxiety was beginning to infect the twins. She's taking the girls and moving back to Ohio to live with her folks."

"Poor Larry."

"He'll only see his girls a few weeks in the summer and at Christmas. He's been walking around the station like a zombie ever since the papers were served."

"And the other two divorces?"

"Jeb Greenlea and David Arden." He leaned back and fixed her with a look that tore at her heart. "Being married to a cop is no picnic. Weird hours, the constant risk of death or injury, not to mention the possibility some creep might take revenge against an arresting officer's family."

"But what about love? Doesn't that count for something?"

His jaw had settled into a hard, unyielding line. "If a cop loves a woman, the best thing he can do for her is keep his distance. Why put someone you love though that kind of hell?"

"You don't think cops should marry?"

"Damn right."

"Look at your mom and dad. They've been happy."

"They had their rough times, but it's worse for today's cops, with more violent criminals, more guns on the streets."

At his explanation of his opposition to marriage, a tiny inner voice badgered her with doubt. If he really loved her, wouldn't he *want* to marry her and work together to deal with the job stress?

She longed to ask which was his greater worry, causing her pain or the fear she'd walk out on him, but she never had the chance to pose the question. Apologizing for spoiling her evening with his foul mood, he'd left immediately.

For several weeks, their relationship returned to what it had been before their lovemaking—until the day she discovered she was pregnant. For her own sake, she had seen him one last time, to sear the memory of him in her heart. If she'd had any doubts about what she planned, recalling his withdrawn and distant behavior the day after Chip was conceived had convinced her.

Dylan viewed marriage and commitment as a prelude to catastrophe. Often she had wondered, if she hadn't become pregnant and removed herself from his life, how long it would have been before Dylan ended their relationship himself.

Affirming the decision she'd made two years ago, she refused now to push him into the very thing he most wanted to avoid. He was so damned *honorable*. If she let him believe she had the slightest feeling for him, he'd insist on marrying her and they'd both end up miserable.

If honor was his hang-up, hers was pride. She loved him with an intensity that robbed her of sleep and breath, but she would never marry him unless he asked her of his own free will, unencumbered by his sense of duty or honor.

Sure, Chip needed a father, but not one alienated and resentful because he'd been forced into marriage by his own high principles.

"We're here," Dylan announced.

With a start, Heather looked up to find the Jeep parked in the Wades' driveway. If Margaret and Frank hadn't already guessed, they wouldn't take long to realize their son was Chip's father. "What will you tell your folks?"

"That Chip's their grandson. They have a right to know."

Heather said nothing. She couldn't argue with the truth.

The screen door opened, and with a welcoming smile, Margaret descended the front steps. She greeted Heather and Dylan and reached for Chip. "Hello, Chipper."

At Margaret's heels, Mame the terrier yapped happily and circled her as she held Chip. Toting luggage, Heather and Dylan followed them inside to the guest room.

Margaret set Chip down and looked at Heather. "Dylan told me on the phone what happened at your house. You poor girl, you're welcome here until things get sorted out and it's safe to return, however long that is."

"Thanks." Heather had always liked Dylan's mom, who had always treated her like one of the family.

"You settle in," Margaret said, "then join me in the kitchen. I made a cake after Dylan called. It'll be coming out of the oven soon."

Her warm hospitality chased away some of Heather's foreboding. "Thank you, Mrs. Wade—"

"Call me Margaret, just like old times." After an encouraging smile, the older woman left the room.

Heather glanced at Dylan, who stood inside the door, studying his son. "You can set my luggage on the bed, please."

As if awakening from a trance, he wrenched his gaze from Chip and lifted the heavy bag onto the quilted coverlet.

Dylan avoided her eyes. "As soon as I've explained to Mother about Chip, I'll leave."

"You'll keep your promise to stay away?" If he

didn't, her resolve might shatter, making her years of sacrifice all for nothing.

This time he faced her, and his expression was undecipherable. "I'll keep out of your way."

Shifting uncomfortably under his gaze, she reached for her luggage and lifted the lid. When she turned toward the closet with an armload of clothes, he was gone.

Relieved he hadn't insisted on more answers about her leaving him, she returned to her unpacking with deliberate slowness, giving him ample opportunity to depart before she carried Chip into the kitchen.

Margaret's blue eyes lit up like Christmas when she saw Chip. "Come to Gramma, sweetheart."

Heather expelled her pent-up breath. "So Dylan told you."

Margaret nodded and lifted Chip into the high chair. "I had already guessed, first time I set eyes on the boy. He may have your eyes and nose, but in every other way, he's a carbon copy of Dylan at that age."

"I'm sorry I couldn't tell you before. I wouldn't blame you for being angry—"

"Don't be silly." Margaret stepped closer and enveloped her in a spontaneous hug. "You did what you thought was best. How can anyone argue with that?"

The short, plump woman smelled of lilacs and sunshine, reminding her of her own mother. "Thank you, and thanks for taking us in again."

"Anytime. After all, you're family." Margaret released her and reached into a cabinet above the counter for blue willow plates. "Now, how about a piece of chocolate cake while it's still warm?"

Margaret's accepting attitude and the sunny kitchen's homey atmosphere provided a buffer against the terrors and anguish of the past two days. Heather sat at the bleached oak table and pushed thoughts of the bearded stranger, her ransacked house and Dylan from her mind. For the first time since her frantic flight to Dylan's house, she believed that maybe things would work out all right.

She and Chip would remain with the Wades until the police caught the kidnapper. If she was lucky, they could return home without encountering Dylan again. Being near him was too dangerous. He stirred the same overpowering emotions in her he always had. If she intended to protect them both from his honorable motives, the sooner she severed all connections, the better.

Margaret's next words fractured her hopes. "Dylan said he'll pick you up at nine tomorrow morning. I told him I'd watch Chip while you're gone."

Heather almost choked on a bite of cake. "Did he say *where* we're going?"

Placidly watching Chip smear chocolate frosting in his hair, Margaret nodded. "He said something about questioning a neighbor of yours, somebody named John."

Chocolate cake turned to sawdust in her mouth. Her appetite and serenity vanished, and she laid down her fork.

She had uncorked the bottle when she'd burst into Dylan's house yesterday, and the genie had escaped. Who knew how much damage he'd do, before she could stuff her rebellious feelings back inside and imprison them again?

DYLAN ARRIVED AT NINE the next morning, appearing at the door of the guest room just as Heather finished dressing Chip after his bath.

"Dyl!" Chip jumped from her grasp and ran toward him.

He scooped Chip in his arms and swung him into the air. The sight of father and son, their faces lit with happiness, pierced her with its sweetness.

"Not Dylan, son. You can call me Daddy." Dylan set the boy back on his feet, but his attention was on Heather. The hardened set of his jaw dared her to contradict him.

"Daddy, Daddy, Daddy." Chip's laughter bubbled through the room, and he gripped Dylan's right knee in a hammerlock.

To avoid a scene, she bit back her objection and stifled the urge to step between them. Nervousness dampened her palms as she struggled to find a way out of her dilemma. Her son's attachment to Dylan was growing too fast, too strong. Since Chip's kidnapping, events had tumbled out of her control, plunging her down a slippery slope with Dylan waiting at its foot.

Margaret's arrival severed her agitated thoughts. "Ready for our trip to the park, Chipper?"

Chip released Dylan's knee. "Go swing, Gramma?"

"The park has swings *and* seesaws, and we can buy popcorn to feed the seagulls." Margaret picked up Chip and turned to Heather. "Frank will meet us when he's through at the hardware store. We'll take good care of Chip."

"Don't count on us for lunch, Mom," Dylan said. "I don't know how long this will take."

Hiding her distress at leaving her son, Heather kissed Chip and followed him and Margaret into the front hall. From the screen door, she watched him and his grandmother walk hand in hand down the oak-shaded street toward the nearby waterfront park.

As soon as they were out of earshot, she whirled, almost bumping into Dylan. She backed up a few steps, placed her hands on her hips and glared at him. "You broke your promise."

He repelled her accusation with a shrug. "You can't have it both ways."

"It?" She narrowed her eyes and tried to ignore how the cadence of her heart accelerated at his nearness.

"We have to work together to find out who's after you. The sooner we find him, the sooner you can go home. Isn't that what you want?"

She wanted a reason to censure and scold, to maintain her distance with angry words, but his logic defused her anger. She attempted to resurrect it. "Why talk to John Rowland? I told you, he's harmless."

"I checked with Officer Parker this morning. He talked with John yesterday and reached the same conclusion, but I want to observe how your neighbor reacts toward you."

She opened her mouth to argue, then realized the futility. "Let's get this over with."

After a tense drive to St. Petersburg with the silence broken only by soft rock on the radio, she stepped out of the Jeep into her driveway.

"Ready?" he asked from the other side of his car.

She nodded. Talking with John Rowland was a colossal waste of time. He'd rant and rave about her oak tree until her stomach was in knots and Velma was in tears, and Dylan would learn nothing. But he obviously wasn't going to leave her alone until he'd interviewed John.

Quickening her pace to keep up with Dylan's long stride, she accompanied him up the brick walk to the neat, two-story clapboard house. Velma Rowland, a rake-thin woman with white hair, answered the door.

"Heather! You haven't had more trouble?" Her watery-blue eyes, owllike behind thick glasses, filled with concern.

Heather smiled and shook her head. Despite her quarrel with John, she and Velma had remained friends. "This is Officer Wade from the Dolphin Bay Police Department. He wants to ask you and John a few questions about yesterday."

"Of course. I remember seeing you visiting Heather often a few years ago." Velma opened the door wide and invited them into a small living room crowded with dark mahogany furniture. "But we already told that nice Officer Parker everything we know."

Dylan flashed her a smile. "Sometimes when a different person asks the questions, people remember something they forgot."

Velma glowed beneath the warmth of Dylan's charm. "Have a seat. John's puttering in his workshop. I'll get him."

Heather selected a wing chair in the corner, as far from Dylan's unsettling presence as she could manage in the tiny room. He stood at the side window, gazing through lace curtains at the unobstructed view of her house.

Footsteps resounded in the hall. John Rowland came into the room and frowned when he saw her. "Changed your mind about that tree, did you?"

"This isn't about the tree," she said, clenching her jaw in her effort at politeness. "Officer Wade has some questions."

John squinted at Dylan in the dim light, and his eyes lit with recognition. "So, you're back. Velma and I figured we'd seen the last of you a couple of years ago."

"Hello, Mr. Rowland," Dylan said. "I'd like to ask a few questions."

John acted as if he hadn't heard. "Back then we thought you'd be moving in permanent next door. A good thing, too, I told Velma. I intended to talk to you about that tree, man to man. Women don't understand such things."

Heather bit her tongue. If John wandered off on that tangent, she and Dylan would be stuck here all morning.

"Too bad you didn't marry her," John continued. "Would have been a good thing, having a man next door. Women are no good in a crisis. If we have a major hurricane—"

"That's why I'm here," Dylan broke in easily. "There's been trouble next door, and we need your help."

She drew back into the shadows of her chair and

studied John while Dylan spoke. The old man *was* about the same height and build as Chip's abductor, and a wig and false beard could have disguised him. The man who had wrenched Chip from her arms had possessed remarkable strength. She recalled the heavy furniture she'd seen John wrestle in his shop in the process of refinishing. Anyone who could manhandle a solid oak highboy could easily overpower her. Shivering, she considered her neighbor in a new light.

"Day before yesterday," Dylan was saying, "how did you spend your morning?"

"Same as yesterday. Same as every day, except Sundays when Velma drags me to mass."

"Can anyone confirm that? I'm not doubting you. Verification is just routine."

She had never witnessed Dylan's interrogation technique. His conciliatory manner placed even the irascible John at ease. Why couldn't Dylan exhibit at least one annoying imperfection, an irritating flaw that would make her love him less?

Dylan flawed?

Why kid herself? She knew the quality of his character. No man deserved her love more than Dylan Wade. But he didn't want her love. At least, not on a permanent basis.

Carrying a tray filled with cups of coffee and a plate of brownies, Velma returned to the room. "Don't look to me for an alibi," she teased her husband. "I've often wondered if, when you're supposed to be in your shop, you haven't sneaked out the alley to the Shuffleboard Club."

Velma's comment jolted Heather upright in her

chair. John Rowland knew her schedule, the make of her car, and could have easily slipped the ransom note through her mail slot without drawing attention. Had his bitterness over their tree dispute pushed him over the edge, made him lash out at her through Chip?

Dylan's contemplative expression suggested he was considering the same possibilities.

Velma set the tray on a low table. "It's lovely to see you, Heather, and to meet your young man, but this is the third time we've answered questions."

"Third?" Dylan raised his eyebrows.

"That's right." John, spurred by a glance from Velma, picked up the plate of brownies and offered it to Heather. "Officer Parker yesterday, the guy earlier this morning and now you."

Forcing herself not to recoil at John's proximity, she reached for a brownie. "Another police officer?"

John shrugged. "That's what I assumed. Come to think of it, he didn't give a name or ID. Said he just wanted to ask about the goings-on next door."

"He was probably the detective working with Officer Parker." She shifted backward in her chair, farther from her neighbor.

"What did he look like?" Dylan asked.

"Casual clothes, sunglasses. Couldn't tell you his age, but he was about my size. You should contact the police department and tell them how to get in touch with you," John told Heather. "This man said he has something for you, but he doesn't know where you've gone. Wanted us to tell him."

Velma shook her head and clucked her tongue. "Poor man, he must have lost all his hair. He was wearing the *homeliest* black wig. Even his beard looked fake.''

The brownie slid from her grasp and, as if in slow motion, floated to the floor, bounced and exploded into crumbs.

Dylan had been right.

The kidnapper wasn't through with her.

Chapter Seven

Dylan watched the color leave Heather's cheeks.

"It was *him*," she said. "For all we know, he's watching the house now, waiting for me."

"The man who broke in yesterday?" Velma asked.

Heather nodded. "The same one who kidnapped Chip the day before."

"Kidnapped Chip?" Velma pressed a quivering hand to her chest. "We didn't know."

"There's not much to tell," Dylan said quickly, before Heather could speak.

Even if the Rowlands weren't suspects, they didn't need to know specific details of the crime. He launched into a censored version of events, while Heather knelt on the rug, sweeping brownie crumbs into a napkin with unsteady fingers.

"I'm sorry for what you've been through," John said to Heather with surprising gentleness when Dylan finished. The grouchiness had vanished from the old man's attitude. "We had a son. He was killed in Vietnam."

Dylan's suspicion of Rowland dissipated when he noted tears in the old man's eyes.

"I lost my son," Rowland said, "and I would never wish that pain on another parent."

My son.

Now Dylan had a son of his own, and his heart swelled with love for his child. Close on its heels came bitterness toward the man who threatened Chip and Heather.

He clamped a lid on feelings that would only hinder his investigation. This morning the Rowlands had spoken face-to-face with the kidnapper. Perhaps they'd noticed a clue that would point to his identity. "Can you tell me anything more about this man who questioned you?"

Velma shook her head. "He refused to come in, and, like we said, his face was covered by a beard and sunglasses."

"What about his arms and hands?" Dylan asked. "Any distinguishing scars, tattoos?"

"Now that you mention it," John said, "it did seem strange he kept his hands in his pockets the whole time."

"And his shirt was long-sleeved," Velma added, "so we couldn't see his arms."

Heather placed her crumb-filled napkin on the tray and dusted her hands. Her composure had returned, and with it, the delicate hues of her complexion. "What about his car? Did you get a license number?"

The Rowlands shook their heads.

"He parked headed into the driveway," John said.

"I couldn't have seen the tag if I'd been looking, but I wasn't. Didn't have a reason to."

"I'm sorry we're not more help." Velma looked ready to cry.

Heather slipped her arm around the woman. "You've helped more than you know."

Dylan ground his teeth, frustrated the kidnapper had been so close, yet eluded them again. "Can you describe the car?"

John nodded. "It was black—"

"Black?" Heather flashed Dylan a look of surprise.

"Did you recognize the make?" Dylan asked.

"Sorry," John said. "I wasn't paying that much attention."

"It was a newer model," Velma added, looking happier now that she had something to contribute, "one of those, oh, what do they call them, John?"

Her husband shrugged. "Beats me."

She wrinkled her forehead as if trying to remember. "They're always driving them through the woods and mud in the TV commercials." Her face brightened. "Like the one you drive, Officer Wade."

"A sport utility vehicle?" Dylan suggested.

"That's it," Velma said. "With tinted windows."

"Mr. and Mrs. Rowland, you've been a big help." He glanced at Heather. "We'd better be going."

"Won't you stay for coffee?" Velma looked disappointed.

Heather hugged the older woman and released her. "Thanks, but I should get back to Chip."

"And I need to alert Officer Parker to what you've told us." Dylan pointed to the window that overlooked Heather's front door. "Keep an eye out in case that guy shows up again. If he does, call the police."

"Where will you be, dear?" Velma asked Heather.

"In a safe place," Dylan said before Heather could reply. "If you need to get in touch, call the Dolphin Bay Police Department. They'll forward your message."

He dug into his pocket, extracted his card and handed it to John Rowland. "Don't approach this guy. Consider him armed and dangerous."

"Thanks again for your help." Heather strode ahead of him to the door.

Dylan stepped outside and scanned the street and driveways of the neighborhood. Not a white car or black sport utility vehicle in sight. Nothing and no one moved on the sleepy residential street.

Except Heather.

In spite of his longer strides, Dylan had to rush to catch up as she raced across the Rowlands' lawn toward her driveway. "Whoa! What's your hurry?"

She circled his Jeep and peered at him over the hood, her eyes luminous with urgency. "Please, take me to Chip. That man's still looking for him."

"Mom and Dad are with him. He'll be fine. Besides, if that creep had any idea where you were, he wouldn't have been hanging around here this morning asking questions."

Dylan stifled the urge to go to her and gather her in his arms, to promise to keep both her and Chip safe. The golden highlights of her hair flashed in the sunlight, and anxiety pinked her cheeks and darkened the exotic green in her eyes. During the past endless, lonely months, he had longed for her with a fierceness worse than torture, but now that she was within reach, circumstances had him as hogtied as a steer in a roping contest.

He could look all he wanted, but not touch. She had clarified her feelings from the start. Not only didn't she love him, she didn't even want him around.

His brain recognized her rejection, but his heart refused the message. Or maybe what his mother called his hardheaded stubbornness made him crave all the more the one woman he couldn't have.

"Get in," he said with a tenderness he couldn't hide. "I'll take you to Chip as soon as I've talked with Officer Parker."

THAT AFTERNOON, Dylan paced his living room like a caged beast during mating season. Taking off from work had been a mistake. Heather had effectively quashed his plans for spending time with his son. After this morning's scare, she didn't want Chip out of her sight, and she had invoked Dylan's earlier promise to leave her alone if she went to his folks.

If he'd had any leads on the identity of the kidnapper, he would have spent the afternoon tracking him, but the only clues he had were sketchy.

After leaving the Rowlands, he and Heather had visited the St. Petersburg PD. Officer Parker had been on patrol, but Detective Cramer, who'd handled the investigation of the break-in at Heather's, had taken the information they'd learned from the Rowlands.

"We still don't have enough to go on," Cramer said when Dylan finished his report.

"I don't understand," Heather said. "I thought you had computers that could collate lists of every white Mercedes and black sport utility vehicle in the county."

Cramer slowly removed his gold-rimmed glasses and polished them carefully with the end of his faded silk tie. Dylan admired the seasoned detective's patience.

"Our computers could do that," Cramer said agreeably, "but there'd be hundreds, maybe thousands, of vehicles from this county alone on that list. It would take more than a dozen officers—which we can't spare—knocking on doors to attempt to identify which car belonged to the kidnapper. And they wouldn't have much luck unless the guy answered the door wearing his wig and fake beard."

"And it's possible," Dylan added, "the kidnapper bought his vehicle at a Tampa, Sarasota or New Port Richey dealership. That adds three more counties and thousands more vehicles to the list—and that's assuming the cars were bought or rented in this part of the state."

"Does that mean there's *nothing* you can do?" Heather asked.

"Not at all. I have a plan." Cramer slid his glasses on. "But I'll need your help."

"Anything. I want the threat to my son ended and this man behind bars."

"I knew I could count on you," Cramer said with an approving grin. "How long will it take to reconstruct your address book?"

"A few hours, maybe. Why?"

"So I can contact your friends," the detective said, "see if the kidnapper visited them, maybe even set up surveillance at a few places."

"I'll work on it this afternoon," Heather promised.

"I'll be in early tomorrow morning. Could I have it then?"

"I'll bring it first thing," Dylan told him.

During the drive back to Dolphin Bay, Dylan had assigned Heather an additional task. "You can make another list that will help the investigation."

"What kind of list?"

"Think back over the past few years and name every person you've had an argument or disagreement with, no matter how trivial it seemed."

"But—"

"I know that you, as a teacher, take pride in your conflict resolution skills, but there has to be *somebody* in the world you've ticked off royally."

"Should I put your name at the top of the list?" Her question held no sarcasm, only sadness.

"I think it's safe to rule me out as a suspect," he said lightly. "But don't omit anyone else—students, faculty members, even the guy who bags your groceries."

She shook her head. The delicate floral fragrance of her shampoo drifted through the vehicle and triggered bittersweet memories.

"Why," she asked, "would someone go to all this trouble over a perceived insult or minor dispute?"

"Some guy shot a motorist in Miami last week, just because she'd cut him off in traffic. There are lots of angry, maladjusted people out there, time bombs waiting to explode. It only takes a tiny spark to light their fuses.''

''That's not a very comforting picture.'' She sighed, as if in resignation. ''I'll make your list, as soon as I've finished the names and addresses for Detective Cramer.''

He had left Heather at his mother's kitchen table, leafing through phone directories for addresses. He had offered to take Chip for the afternoon, but she had refused, insisting Chip needed his nap.

Frustrated at being denied time with his son, Dylan had returned home and paced his living room instead.

Abruptly he stopped in the center of the room. Once the kidnapper was caught and Heather returned home, would she allow him to see his son? Anger and resentment boiled inside him. She had already stolen almost two years of Chip's childhood. Dylan intended to guarantee that she couldn't deprive him further of his right to share and influence his son's life.

What he needed was a lawyer.

Dolphin Bay boasted three excellent law firms, but reluctant to share his private dilemma with strangers, he punched the number of Sinclair and Moore Construction into his phone.

The receptionist answered, and he asked for Rand Sinclair.

''Mr. Sinclair is out of the office for the rest of the day.''

''This is Officer Dylan Wade, Dolphin Bay police.'' His conscience pricked only slightly at the pretense of police business. ''Where can I find him?''

"Mr. Sinclair is on the construction site of the new shopping mall, on the main highway just north of the county line."

"Thanks."

He grabbed his keys from the tray beside the front door and sprinted for his Jeep.

As he drove north along the traffic-choked highway, Dylan began to relax. If anyone could help him, Rand Sinclair could. They'd been as close as brothers since childhood, and only last year, Dylan had arrested the man who'd threatened Jasmine Ross, now Rand's wife. Dylan had been there for Rand during those tough times, and he was positive Rand would return the favor.

Thirty minutes later, Dylan turned off the highway onto a sandy road cut through a stand of cypress trees to a multiacre clearing a hundred yards from the asphalt. Bulldozers and other heavy equipment ripped undergrowth from the ground and shoved uprooted trees and other debris into piles. Noise, diesel fumes and dust filled the air.

Before clearing had begun, the site had been a quiet enclave of dense forest amid creeping urbanization. Dylan couldn't avoid a comparison with his own life. Before Heather showed up again, his existence had been relatively calm. Not perfect or particularly happy, but at least undisturbed. In a matter of days, she had changed his life as radically as Rand's heavy equipment had altered the construction site. Now Dylan was determined to create some alterations of his own.

Jostling over the makeshift road, he headed toward the other side of the clearing, where a huge trailer beneath an ancient live oak bore the Sinclair and Moore Construction logo. He parked beside Rand's car at the on-site office and strode to the front door.

"Come in," Rand yelled in answer to his knock.

A blast of air-conditioned air greeted him as he stepped into the mobile office. Rand Sinclair stood behind a draftsman's table covered with blueprints. Dressed in casual slacks and a chambray shirt with sleeves rolled to his elbows, his tall, rugged friend looked more like a construction foreman than head of his own multimillion-dollar company. His face split into a welcoming grin when he saw Dylan.

"What brings you all the way out here? Did I lose the bet on the All-Star game?"

Dylan stopped short. Heather had him so distracted, not only had he missed the game, he hadn't caught the final score. "Who won?"

Rand's smile vanished. He laid down his pencil and motioned Dylan into a chair beside the desk. "I'm the one who's supposed to be absentminded these days, but you're in worse shape than I am. What's going on?"

Rand sank into his desk chair, laced his fingers behind his head and scrutinized Dylan with a concentration that made him antsy. Face-to-face with his oldest and best buddy, he was suddenly reluctant to talk about his problems.

"You first. How's Jasmine?"

"Terrific, as always. Only four weeks before the baby arrives." Rand's expression darkened. "But she's worried about her mother."

"Is Lily ill?"

Rand shook his head. "Remember what I told you

six weeks ago, about Lily and Talbot discovering they had another child?''

"Uh-huh." Lily's kid had been born nine months after Charles Wilcox imprisoned Lily in the nursing home. *Kid* wasn't exactly the right word. The unknown male or female would be twenty-something now.

"The search reached a dead end, and it's breaking Lily's heart."

"Charles won't tell them where he sent the child?"

"He claims he doesn't know anything about it. He does, but he refuses to incriminate himself by telling us."

"He's already locked up for the rest of his life. What's he got to lose?"

"Charles, the mean bastard," Rand said, "is taking great pleasure in Talbot and Lily's misery. He blames them for his crimes."

"Charles is a classic psychopath." Dylan recalled the case that had rocked the town less than a year ago. "Nothing's ever *his* fault."

"Everybody knows Charles was in the wrong," Rand said with a scowl. "I don't understand how he can maintain he's not to blame."

"Take it from one who's arrested plenty of psychopaths, you don't understand because you don't *think* like they do. From Charles' point of view, everything *is* Talbot and Lily's fault."

"How can he believe that?" Rand asked.

"According to Charles, if Lily hadn't existed, he wouldn't have been forced to remove her as his sister's rival. If Talbot and Jasmine had conveniently died, Charles wouldn't have attempted to murder them to gain control of your and Talbot's company.''

"Only over my dead body," Rand snapped.

"Charles would have been happy to accommodate. In fact, I'm surprised he didn't try." Still unready to talk about himself, Dylan launched a new tack. "How's business?"

Rand waved toward the construction site. "Couldn't be better, in spite of Talbot's spending less time in the office. T.J. and Art are doing a good job of filling their father's shoes."

"And Blain?"

"Living in France with his mother. Which is just as well. He's the baby of the family, and he's acting like one. He still isn't ready to forgive Talbot for divorcing Irene." Rand squinted at Dylan with an inquisitive stare. "You didn't drive all this way just to ask about Jasmine and the Moores. What's up?"

Attempting nonchalance, Dylan propped his right ankle on his left knee and fiddled with the laces of his running shoe. "Looks like I beat you to fatherhood, old buddy."

"What?" Rand bolted upright and slammed his feet to the floor. Under other circumstances, the shock on his face would have been comical.

Dylan shrugged. "Heather has an eighteen-month-old boy."

"He's yours?"

"Heather says so."

"Then it's true. Heather wouldn't lie." Next to Dylan, Rand had always been Heather's biggest fan.

"I never figured she'd dump me, either, but she did, as soon as she discovered she was pregnant."

"Did she explain why she left?"

Dylan grimaced. "She was afraid I would've insisted on marrying her."

"You would have."

"You're right. And she undoubtedly didn't want to marry me, so she ended it."

Rand opened his mouth as if to say something, then clamped it shut. After a moment, he spoke. "I take it you're not here to pass out cigars."

"I need legal advice."

Rand held up his hands in protest. "I don't practice, remember? I went straight from law school into Talbot's business."

Dylan pushed to his feet, walked to the window and gazed out across the dusty clearing. "You graduated summa cum laude. You must remember something about custody cases from your law studies."

Rand jumped to his feet. "You're not planning to take the child away from his mother?"

"He's my son, too!" Dylan forced himself to relax. Yelling at his best friend would get him nowhere. "All I want is visitation rights."

"Have you asked Heather?"

Dylan shoved his hands in his back pockets. "What's the use? She's made it plenty damn clear she doesn't want me around her or Chip."

"His name's Chip?"

"Dylan Wade Taylor. Chip's his nickname."

"As in 'chip off the old block'?" With a contemplative frown, Rand sank into his chair. "I think you're selling Heather short."

"Give me a break. I know 'drop dead' when I hear it."

"How come she gave the child *your* name if she hates you so much?"

Dylan flung his hands up in frustration. "Look, I just want to make sure I can spend time with Chip on a regular basis. In my job, I deal with too many kids whose lives are screwed up by absentee fathers. I don't want that happening to my son."

"You want my advice?"

"That's why I'm here."

"Talk to Heather."

Dylan regarded his friend with disbelief. "You're out of your mind. She'll refuse."

"You're angry now—and with good cause," Rand said with irritating reasonableness. "I would be, too, in your situation. But anger is clouding your thinking."

Dylan scowled. "You bet I'm angry, but not so angry I can't feel the boot on my butt when I'm being kicked out the door."

"Give it time. After you've cooled off, discuss visitation rights with Heather. If she refuses to co-operate, which I doubt, then I'll recommend an attorney."

"You might as well give me the name now and save me another trip."

"You'll hurt your case if you don't try working things out with Heather first." Rand tugged his wallet out of his back pocket and drew out a five-dollar bill. "By the way, you won that bet on the All-Star game."

"Keep it, as payment for your advice." Dylan crossed the room and paused in the doorway. "It's ten times what it was worth."

He slammed the door on his way out, but not before catching the look of sympathy on Rand's face.

"WAIT HERE WHILE I CHECK inside." Dylan took the house key from Heather. Leaving her on the porch, he made a hurried sweep of her empty house and returned. "All clear. You can come in now."

He stepped aside to allow her to pass, and gripped the door frame to keep from reaching for her. His longing to hold her burned like a thirst nothing could quench. A good night's sleep, the result of his exhaustion, had sharpened his physical responses. Every nerve ending longed for reciprocal contact with her, whose body he knew by heart, like the well-read pages of a much-loved book.

Anger didn't help. His resentment at her abandonment and deception and his disgust with himself over yesterday's quarrel with Rand only fueled his tension. He should have put his foot down when she insisted on accompanying him this morning and saved himself this agony.

When he had arrived at his parents' to pick up Heather's reconstructed address list for Cramer, she had been adamant about going home to gather more clothes and toys for Chip. Since he had forced her to abandon her car, he had little choice but to yield to her demand.

He hoped Cramer would find her list of names and addresses helpful. The sooner the kidnapper was caught, the sooner Dylan's misery would end. The numb emptiness of life without Heather had been easier to bear than the torture of self-imposed restraint in her presence.

Rousing himself from his thoughts, he found her watching him, her green eyes guarded. He hastily closed and locked the door from the inside. "Will this take long?"

"I'm going to make coffee. Your mother had only decaf this morning, and I need the caffeine to stave off a headache."

He suppressed a groan of desire. Coffee wasn't what he wanted. "Forget the coffee. We promised Cramer your list early today."

"It won't take long. While it brews, we can discuss the list *you* asked me to make."

He didn't want to *discuss* anything. He wanted to scoop her in his arms, carry her down the hall to her poster bed, as he'd done only once before but hundreds of times in his dreams, and make love to her until they were both too weak to move.

"The sooner you catch this guy," she said, "the sooner Chip and I will be out of your hair."

Had he lost his mind? He didn't want them out of his hair. He wanted to spend all his days with Heather and his son. Except for one small but insurmountable problem. If he disappeared instantly in a puff of smoke, it wouldn't be too soon for Heather.

He trailed behind her into the kitchen and sat at the table. "Who are your suspects?"

"It isn't a long list." She removed a paper from her pocket, handed it to him and, with characteristic efficiency, started coffee brewing.

He unfolded the legal-size sheet, and his eyes bulged. "Fourteen!"

"I did what you asked." She leaned against the

counter, arms folded, her bottom lip caught between her teeth.

He had nibbled those lips many times, and the memory of the taste of her blossomed in his mouth. He swallowed hard and concentrated on the list.

"How did you manage to tick off more than a dozen people? I remember a lot of things about you, but terminally obnoxious isn't one of them."

"Thank you. I think."

She slipped onto the chair beside him and pointed to the list. Her breast brushed his arm, sending pleasure signals straight to his groin, making him glad the table hid his taut lower body from view. He wouldn't give her the satisfaction of knowing he wanted her, that her slightest touch rendered him hard with need.

"These top three are the only people I've had *serious* disagreements with."

"We've pretty much eliminated John Rowland." He drew a line through the first name on the list. "Who's Robert Tipton?"

She sighed and leaned back in her chair, breaking the contact that had battered his senses. "He's the father of one of my students."

"You argued with him?"

She nodded. "He was really hot. Three weeks ago, I thought he was going to jump across my desk and throttle me."

"Why didn't you mention him before?"

"Because I'd forgotten all about him until last night. His daughter Kayla was in my honors history class this year."

"Did you fail her?"

"Might as well have, from the way her dad reacted. She earned a B."

Dylan squeezed his eyes shut and tried to concentrate. "Her dad reamed you out because his daughter made a B in your class? A bit obsessive, isn't he?"

"She was three points below an A. He said I should have given her the extra points. The B in history ruined her eligibility for valedictorian of her class."

"Three points doesn't seem like a big deal. Why did you refuse?"

"Because Kayla could have achieved that A herself if she'd bothered to turn in homework assignments. The kids on the list for valedictorian *earned* their places. Giving Kayla points she didn't deserve wouldn't have been fair to the others."

Heather had always carried fairness to a fault, which made her keeping Chip's existence from him so hard to understand. "So her father threatened you?"

"He swore if I didn't raise her grade, he'd have me fired."

"An empty threat?"

"Maybe, but Robert Tipton is a wealthy and influential man with several friends on the school board."

"What happened then?"

"Nothing. I told him if the board wanted to fire me for doing my job, I didn't really want to work for them, anyway."

"And that was that?"

She nodded. "I didn't see him again. He spoke

with my principal, but she backed my decision, and that was the last I heard of the incident.''

"I think we'd better pay a call on Tipton. He could be the type who's lashing back at you and Chip because he believes you hurt his kid.'' Dylan circled Tipton's name. "Who's Andrew Hayward?''

"Lea's husband. Lea's a good friend who teaches in my department.''

"What's Hayward's beef?''

A bright flush flooded her face. "He claims I'm interfering in their marriage.''

"Are you?''

"Yes.'' She rose and filled two mugs with coffee.

"How?''

She turned and met his gaze with unblinking eyes. "I encouraged Lea to divorce him.''

He wasn't surprised. Heather had walked out on him easily enough. Little wonder she had urged her friend to do the same.

She handed him a mug, stirred cream and sugar in her coffee and settled back at the table. "Andy was abusive.''

"He hit her?''

"His mistreatment was emotional, not physical. Andy Hayward is a control freak. Lea couldn't take a breath without his permission. If she crossed him, he punished her with cold, disapproving silence. He was undermining her self-esteem and making her life miserable. I suggested she get out.''

"Do they have kids?''

She shook her head. "They married last year. When they were dating, Lea used to say how attentive Andy was. She didn't see his attentiveness as a form of control until after the wedding.''

He had answered enough domestic complaints to recognize the truth in Heather's assessment. No woman should be a doormat for any man.

You never treated Heather that way, so why did she leave you?

He ignored the nasty voice in his head. "Did Andy threaten you?''

She placed her mug on the table and ran her fingers through her hair. "He stormed into my classroom one day after school, screaming and hollering that he'd kill me if I didn't stay away from Lea and quit feeding her ideas.''

The hair rose on the back of his neck. "Why didn't you report this to the police?''

"Because he apologized.''

"What?''

Her face crinkled in a self-deprecating smile. "After I screamed and hollered back at him.''

His jaw dropped.

"I called him a petty little dictator and told him, after the way he'd treated Lea, he deserved to lose her.''

"And he just backed down?''

"After I called his bluff. I told him if he ever burst into my classroom and threatened me again, I'd file criminal *and* civil charges.'' Her eyes flashed with remembered fury.

This was the Heather of his memory, queen of spunk, champion of the underdog, exactly the kind of person who might send a control freak like Hayward into a murderous rage. "Maybe we should let Cramer deal with Lea's husband."

"Lea's soon-to-be *ex*-husband. She filed for divorce when she learned how he'd threatened me. His tantrum opened her eyes."

He drained the last of his coffee. "Which gives Hayward an even stronger motive for hurting you."

"Andy Hayward is all hot air. He doesn't have the guts to do anything more than threaten." Heather picked up his mug and hers and rinsed them in the sink.

"What about these others on the list?"

She turned and reached for a hand towel. At the same instant, the window behind her exploded in a hail of shattered glass.

Chapter Eight

Heather dropped to the floor when the window exploded. Dylan dived after her, covering her with his body as more shots whined overhead.

When the barrage of bullets ended, he eased off her and ran his hands over her face and through her hair. "Are you hit?"

If she was, she was too stunned to detect it. When he withdrew his hands, she saw blood, and a sudden light-headedness seized her.

"I don't *feel* anything," she said weakly. Her statement wasn't entirely true. In spite of shock and terror, she had registered every burning contact with his body, every tingling sensation of his hands' exploration.

Drawing her head against his chest, he lifted her hair and skimmed his fingers across the back of her neck. "It's just a scratch. You were hit by flying glass."

He shifted to tug a handkerchief from his pocket, and the pressure of his hips against hers sent her already giddy senses reeling. Gently, he pressed the folded linen against the cut on her neck, then wriggled against her again to take out his phone and crush it into her free hand.

"Call the police. Then crawl to the hall closet and stay there until I come back."

"Don't leave." She choked back a sob. Outside waited a man with a gun. Dylan would be barging into his sights.

"You'll be safe. Call 911, *now*."

One instant he was there, his warmth a bulwark against terror. The next, he was gone. With unsteady fingers, she punched in the emergency number and reported the shooting, then scurried in a crouch up the hallway into the closet and closed the door.

Waiting in the darkness with the phone jammed to her ear, she realized Dylan had misinterpreted her plea for him to stay. He had assumed she was afraid and wanted his protection. She couldn't deny that, but keeping him safe had been her overriding motivation.

The brief moment of physical closeness, the scorching heat of his body, the warmth of his breath and the euphoria of his arms around her had reminded her with cruel clarity of all she had lost.

She loved him. She would always love him, and the possibility he might be injured, or worse, filled her with numbing despair. While she prayed for his safety, long minutes dragged by.

"Ma'am?" The 911 operator spoke in her ear. "The cruiser's at your house now. The officers are coming inside."

Vibrations in the floorboards communicated approaching footsteps. The police had arrived, but where was Dylan? He should have returned by now.

Anxiety, thicker than the closet's inky darkness, seized her.

"Heather, it's me," Dylan called from the other side of the door. "It's safe to come out now."

The closet door opened and he reached for her. With a sob of relief, she leaped from the floor and flung her arms around him. "Thank God, you're all right."

He clasped her in his arms, and she buried her face in his neck. Time stopped as she inhaled his familiar, cherished scent, and her body, fired by his heat, molded to his. She tossed back her head and lifted her lips. A peripheral glimpse of a female officer waiting in the hall brought her to her senses.

Heather stiffened and shoved away. In her joy at seeing him unhurt, the inhibitions that protected her had dissipated. Letting him know she still cared was courting disaster, and she had more than enough trouble already.

To avoid his puzzled gaze, she knelt in the closet to retrieve his handkerchief, which she'd dropped when he opened the door. After composing her features, she faced him again. If her display of emotion had affected him, his expression didn't show it.

"Did you catch him?" she asked.

He shook his head. "If he used a rifle with a scope, he could have shot from anywhere—a tree, a roof. Wherever he was, he's gone now."

Detective Cramer barged in the open front door and muttered something to the female officer, who turned and left. He approached Heather. "You okay?"

"As soon as my adrenaline level drops to normal so I can stop shaking."

She avoided Dylan's gaze. He bore as much responsibility for her spike in adrenaline as the sniper, but she would never admit it. Better for him to suspect she'd thrown herself at him in hysteria.

The female officer returned. "All clear around back now."

Cramer acknowledged the report with a nod and turned to Dylan. "Let's check the damage."

Dylan led the way to the kitchen, and Heather followed the detective. When she spotted the destruction the rifle slugs had inflicted on the pantry door and realized what the bullets could have done to her, her knees threatened to buckle. She sagged into the nearest chair while Dylan and Cramer studied the room.

They measured the trajectory of the bullets, one of which had lodged in a roll of paper towels on the pantry shelf, and established that the shots had been fired from the second floor of an unoccupied house across the alley. Cramer dispatched an officer to search the building.

After taking Polaroid shots of the shattered window and pantry, he placed the recovered slugs in a plastic evidence bag and turned to her. "Do you have those names and addresses you promised me?"

She shook splinters of glass from the papers she had abandoned on the table and handed them to him.

"Heather also drew up a list of potential suspects," Dylan said. "Since you're shorthanded, I'm volunteering to interview the top three."

"Your department is also on this case, so your

involvement won't violate policy.'' Cramer's face creased in a speculative frown. ''In the last twenty-four hours, I've had a murder-suicide, a DUI homicide and a drive-by shooting added to my caseload. I can really use the help.''

''I want this guy caught,'' Dylan said.

She shuddered at the ferocity of his expression. He'd neglected to tell Cramer that he was on vacation and officially off duty. Before, he had always operated by the book. His willingness to circumvent procedure proved his determination to nab Chip's kidnapper.

Cramer stuffed his notebook and her lists into his shirt pocket. ''I'm finished here. Take care of yourself, Ms. Taylor.''

Dylan walked the detective to the door, and she swept broken glass and dumped it in the trash. When she finished, she looked up to find Dylan watching her from the doorway. His stoic expression revealed nothing of his thoughts, but the heat in his eyes spoke volumes.

''Come here,'' he said.

She replaced the broom and dustpan in the pantry and crossed the room, expecting to follow him up the hall and out the front door.

But he took her by the shoulders and directed her toward the bathroom.

''What are you doing?''

''Tending to that cut on your neck.''

She tried to wrest free of his grasp. ''It'll be okay—''

''Let me be the judge of that.''

He held her fast and shoved her gently into the

bathroom. After turning on the fluorescent light, he lifted her hair away from her neck. The combination of cool air and warm fingers on her nape raised goose bumps.

"The cut needs cleaning," he said.

She stared at the shower where that one night eons ago, she and Dylan had indulged in long, passionate lovemaking beneath the steaming spray. Her adrenaline surged again, speeding her respiration and pulse. If he touched her once more, she wouldn't be able to hide her longing.

She whipped around to face him. "I'll take care of it."

"Don't be silly. You can't see what you're doing back there."

He hovered with his face inches above hers, and her gaze locked with the molten brown of his eyes, reflecting her desire.

"God help me," he said with a groan. Tangling his fingers in her hair, he lowered his mouth to hers.

Unable to stop herself, she returned the pressure of his kiss, reveling in the familiar taste of him, heady as her favorite wine. The curves of her body conformed to his with the effortless ease of remembrance, as if their perfect fit had been imprinted on her brain.

Every cell in her body sparked with exquisite need when he glided his fingers across her shoulders, down the length of her arms and grasped her bottom, pulling her closer, blasting the last barricades of her resistance.

Intoxicated with desire, she explored the planes and contours of his back, soaked in his beloved heat through her palms, her breasts, the tops of her thighs. Giddy from the taste and feel of him, she yielded to the urgency of his lips and hands and abandoned all conscious thought, aware only of tactile pleasures.

Abruptly, he released her and stepped away. The remorse etched on his face doused her passion.

"I'm sorry." His heavy, ragged breathing was amplified in the small room. "It won't happen again."

He leaned over the sink and splashed cold water on his face, while she straightened her clothes, rumpled by his roaming hands. She should feel grateful he'd stopped them from going further. Their lovemaking might bring them transitory pleasure, but it wouldn't change things. It would only make returning to life without him harder.

Dylan had stated emphatically he wasn't the marrying kind. If he offered marriage for Chip's sake, passion might sustain their relationship temporarily, but eventually resentment would set in. He would feel trapped, and she and Chip would bear the brunt of his misery, whether they continued to live with an unhappy Dylan or their forced union succumbed to divorce.

Undeniable heartache awaited her at the end of a walk down the aisle.

She had recognized the futility of continuing their relationship when she left Dylan two years ago. The only difference in their situation now was that a killer stalked her and her son. She had to focus on keeping Chip safe and convince herself nothing else mattered.

"What are we going to do?" she asked.

"About what?" He lowered his towel to reveal a

face once more composed. The earlier heat had faded from his eyes, replaced by a glint of wariness.

"About finding the man who shot at me."

He replaced the towel on its rack and reached into the medicine cabinet for Band-Aids and ointment. With an efficient but dispassionate touch, he cleaned and dressed the wound on her neck. Faking an equally impersonal demeanor, she surrendered to his care.

With her cut clean and covered, he replaced the first aid supplies, left the bathroom and strode up the hall.

"Why won't you answer my question?" she called after him.

"*I'm* going to question Robert Tipton and Andrew Hayward and find out where they were this morning," he called over his shoulder. "*You're* going back to my parents' house."

She hastened to catch up. "I'm coming with you."

He stopped so abruptly, she ran into him. He swiveled, glowering. "No way. I'm taking you back to Dolphin Bay."

She stiffened and drew herself to her full height. "Why shouldn't I come? I know these men. I can tell better than you whether their actions seem suspicious or abnormal."

"Forget it."

"If I'm there, you can observe how they react to *me*. Their responses might give them away."

His angry frown switched to thoughtfulness, and the obstinate line of his jaw softened. "I'll probably regret this, but come on. Just let me do the talking."

FOLLOWING HEATHER'S directions, Dylan turned his Jeep west toward Tyrone Mall. "You're sure Hayward still lives in the same place?"

She nodded. "Lea moved into an apartment, and Andy kept the house. When I spoke with her a few days ago, she said he might have to sell. He's been laid off work."

"His wife leaves and he loses his job, all in a matter of weeks. He sounds like he might be desperate."

If Andy Hayward was as unstable as Heather's description indicated, he might attempt to hurt her. Dylan would have to stay alert.

"Andy has problems, but he's brought them all on himself," she said, not unkindly. "He's a perfect example of a person with a superiority complex."

"Which is usually a cover-up for poor self-esteem. Why don't I take you back to Chip?" Concerned for her safety, he used Chip to entice her away from danger.

"Chip's in seventh heaven with your mother. I've never seen two people bond so quickly." The sudden radiance of her smile shattered his detachment. "He'll be fine without me for a few more hours."

He jerked his attention to oncoming traffic. Earlier, he'd allowed his desire to take control. He wouldn't commit such a slip again. The pain of her desertion festered like an unhealed wound, and he'd been a fool to act as if he still cared. She was probably laughing inside at his sentimentality.

But she kissed me as if she enjoyed it.

She'd just been shot at, for crying out loud, he argued with himself. She was scared and needed comforting. Hell, under those circumstances, maybe she'd have even kissed Cramer. He'd known people who'd done stranger things under stress.

"Take a right at the next corner," she instructed.

He turned onto a narrow street lined with stuccoed houses in pastel shades. Fierce late morning sun reflected off the white roofs and shriveled the neatly trimmed lawns.

When she directed him to pull over near the end of the block, Hayward's house with its peeling paint and unkempt yard stood out like a coal lump in a jewel box. If people's homes reflected their state of mind, Andy Hayward was one unhappy puppy.

Dylan climbed from the Jeep and surveyed the area with a cop's eye. In the open carport, a dark maroon sport utility vehicle was parked.

Heather followed his glance. "It looks almost black in the shade."

He nodded tensely. "Stay behind me. I'll do the talking."

With her dogging his footsteps, he approached the front door. Voices from a television blared through the door's open jalousie windows. He rang the bell and the sound ceased immediately.

"Yeah, whaddaya want?" A man with tousled hair and an unshaven face scowled through the open jalousies.

Dylan removed his shield from his pocket and held it close to the door. "Officer Dylan Wade, Dolphin Bay police. Are you Andrew Hayward?"

The man grunted. "What do the Dolphin Bay police want with me?"

"We're investigating a series of crimes, Mr. Hayward, and I want to ask you some questions. May I come in?''

''What the hell, might as well. Ain't a damn thing on television now.''

Hayward jerked the door open and noticed Heather for the first time. Hatred glazed his eyes, and his lips twisted in a sneer.

''What are *you* doing here? Did you bring the cop? For your information, Ms. Buttinsky, I haven't violated Lea's restraining order.''

''I—'' she began, but Dylan cut her off.

''Ms. Taylor is just along for the ride.'' He noted Hayward's medium height and build, the same as the kidnapper's. ''She's a member of our citizen observer program.''

''Right, and I'm John Kennedy Jr.''

''Do you have a problem with her being here?'' Dylan asked. ''She can wait in the car.''

Heather scorched him with a withering look, but he ignored her and riveted his attention to every nuance of Andy Hayward's expression and movement.

''Bring her in,'' Andy said with a shrug. ''Let's get this over with.''

He stood aside for Dylan and Heather to enter. The front door opened directly into his living room with frayed upholstered furniture and scarred tables littered with newspapers, beer cans and discarded pizza boxes.

Dylan and Heather stood and waited until Andy had settled on the sofa.

''Where were you earlier this morning?'' Dylan began.

"I already told you that I haven't violated the restraining order. The judge would throw me in jail."

"This isn't about a restraining order." Dylan caught sight of a tall gun cabinet at the back of the room and injected his voice with friendly interest. "Hey, you like guns, too?"

"Yeah. They're my hobby."

"Mine, too," Dylan lied, "but on a cop's salary, I can't afford them. Mind if I take a look?"

Andy shed his belligerent, hangdog expression. "Help yourself. You a hunter?"

"No." Dylan opened the cabinet's glass door for a better view of the rack of target rifles. "Never liked bloodshed. Target shooting is my interest."

Heather said nothing, and Dylan hoped Andy wasn't watching her, because her face registered bewilderment at his lies.

Dylan removed a Remington Model 700 with a scope, held it to his shoulder and pretended to take aim out the front window. "This is a great piece."

"That's my favorite," Andy said. "I bought it right before...a few weeks ago."

Dylan opened the bolt and sniffed. "Smells like it hasn't been cleaned since it was last fired. Did you shoot it this morning?"

Andy's uneasy expression returned. "Yeah, what of it?"

"Nothing." Dylan shrugged, slid the gun back in its cabinet and made a mental note of the make and caliber of the other rifles. "Just wondered where you practice."

"The police range in Tampa."

Dylan remembered the pistol cartridges retrieved

in the packing house. "Do you ever shoot hand-guns?"

"Nope. Don't even own one. I prefer rifles."

Dylan closed the cabinet. "Do you shoot alone or compete with a group?"

"Alone, especially during the week. I try to beat my own score."

Dylan moved closer to Heather, who stood quietly, eyeing Andy as prey views a predator. "Where were you yesterday morning and the morning before that?"

"At the rifle range, like every day since I lost my job." Andy's face hardened into ugly lines, and he shot a hate-filled gaze at Heather. "What's this all about? Has Lea been complaining about me?"

"Can anyone at the range vouch for your presence?" Dylan asked.

"How should I know? I go to shoot, not chitchat. What's going on?"

"I'm investigating a kidnapping and attempted murder," Dylan said.

"Attempted murder!" Andy blanched and comprehension lit his eyes. "With a rifle?"

Dylan nodded.

Andy licked his lips and clasped his shaking hands beneath his armpits. "Look, man, I got enough trouble between my wife leaving and losing my job. I swear, I'm not mixed up in any murder attempt."

"Then you don't have anything to worry about," Dylan said. "We won't take any more of your time."

He grasped Heather's elbow and steered her ahead of him out of the house.

When they were halfway to the car, Hayward called from the front door. "Heather?"

She turned, and Dylan tensed, ready to throw himself between her and any harm Andy could inflict.

"Please," he whined. "Tell Lea I miss her."

Heather's expression was a collage of pity, anger and disgust. "I'll tell her."

"Do you think Andy was the one who shot at me?" Heather asked over lunch at an outdoor table of a fast-food restaurant.

Dylan shrugged. "He had motive and opportunity, but I'll reserve judgment until I've seen the ballistics report on the slugs taken from your kitchen."

"What if the slugs are the same caliber as Andy's rifle?"

"Along with the threats Andy made to you, Cramer might have cause for a warrant to confiscate the gun for testing."

The first throbs of a tension headache drummed behind her eyes. Her earlier attempt to circumvent the attack with coffee hadn't succeeded. Emotional strain and the unaccustomed chaos in her life were taking their toll. She set aside her half-eaten salad, dug aspirin from her purse and swallowed them with the last of her iced tea.

"You sure you're up to another interview?" he asked.

"I'm sure. The sooner we find out who's behind all this, the sooner my life and Chip's can return to normal."

Normal meant without Dylan, but she could endure the chronic, aching loneliness better than her unblunted desire to throw herself in his arms.

"Sounds as if you've been happy with that life." His tone was neutral, and she couldn't read the expression in his eyes, hidden by the reflective lenses of his sunglasses.

"Motherhood agrees with me." That much, at least, was true. "What about you? Is Clyde Heller still your partner?"

A sudden and ominous stillness settled over him. "Clyde's dead. Eight months ago."

Shock robbed her temporarily of speech. A year younger than Dylan, the fun-loving, wisecracking Clyde had ridden with him for years. "What happened?"

"We responded to an alarm at a convenience store. Three kids, teenagers, hopped up on drugs, had robbed it. We met them coming out. One of them panicked and shot Clyde in the face."

Her stomach twisted in horror. "Did they shoot you?"

"They tried to take me out, but my vest stopped their bullets." His tone remained flat, but a muscle ticking in his jaw transmitted his distress. "Clyde hung on for six weeks, but he never regained consciousness."

"How are Annie and the kids coping?"

"They have Clyde's pension and life insurance, but Annie still cries at the mention of his name. Her boys are having trouble sleeping and problems in school."

"It seems so unfair."

"We arrested the shooters, but they're juveniles.

They'll be back on the street before they're my age.''
Bitterness tainted his voice.

"Maybe I can visit Annie when we return to Dolphin Bay."

He nodded. "She always liked you. Seeing you might cheer her up."

She blinked back tears. "Poor Annie."

"I warned Clyde," Dylan said flatly.

"About the robbery?"

"About marriage. Police marriages don't last. If divorce doesn't break them, death does. He should never have married Annie." His voice implied more torment than censure. "He ruined her life."

Anger stripped away her sadness. "How can you say that?"

"Because it's true."

She leaned toward him, tense with indignation. "Clyde *loved* Annie. In the grand scheme of things, even if he hadn't been a cop, he might have died young, hit by a car or struck down by disease. At least this way, he and Annie had several years of happiness together before his death. And Annie has her children and her memories."

He set his jaw in the stubborn pose she remembered with such clarity. "I wonder if she considers those memories worth the pain."

"Have you asked her?"

He flinched, as if shocked by the question. "No."

"Then maybe you should." Fury, too long suppressed, over the attitude that had driven her away, unleashed her tongue. "No marriage comes with guarantees. Loving is always a risk, because, sooner or later, we're all terminal."

"Since when are you a fatalist?"

"I'm a realist," she countered. "Yes, Clyde died young. If he'd lived to the ripe old age of eighty and they'd been together sixty years, do you think Annie would hurt any less when he died?"

Did he really believe cops shouldn't marry, or was his conviction a smoke screen for his reluctance to commit himself? She longed to rip the sunglasses from his face to expose the look in his eyes.

As if reading her thoughts, he pulled off his glasses and hooked them onto the neckline of his shirt. His gaze, filled with pain and uncertainty, met hers. "I never considered that angle."

Her outburst had depleted her anger, and embarrassment filled the void. Twice today she'd lost control, once through desire, again through anger. Harrowing circumstances were loosening her grip.

"Sorry about the lecture. Since I was shot at this morning, my emotions have been running riot."

"Considering what you've been through, your composure is remarkable." His compliment made her blush. "Ready to tackle Robert Tipton?"

Relieved at the change of subject, she nodded. "I looked in the pay phone directory while you were ordering. Tipton isn't listed, but the school office will have his address."

"Do you want to phone for it?"

"School's only a couple of blocks away. I can check my faculty mailbox and get the address at the same time."

During the short drive to the school, Dylan remained unusually quiet, but she couldn't worry whether her comments on love and marriage had offended him. They had needed saying. If she'd been smarter, she would have cleared the air between them on the subject before she'd withdrawn from his life.

He pulled the Jeep into the faculty parking lot of the low, modern building and followed her into the school's administrative offices.

Darlene Winburn, the school secretary, a willowy redhead with a predominant overbite, rose from her desk and approached the counter when they entered.

"Thank God you're here. I've been calling your house for the last two hours."

"Chip?" Heather asked anxiously.

"No, honey, it's not about Chip." Darlene's eyes widened in surprise when she spotted Dylan with Heather, but she quickly recovered her composure. "Someone was here earlier, asking how to locate you on a matter of life and death."

"A bearded man, medium height?" Dylan said.

"You remember Dylan Wade?" Heather asked Darlene.

Darlene inclined her head in recognition. "The person looking for Heather was a woman."

"A woman?" Heather thought immediately of Margaret Wade and her anxiety over Chip returned, until she remembered Margaret could have reached them on Dylan's mobile phone. "Did she give her name or say what the urgent matter was?"

"She wouldn't tell me anything. Just kept insisting she had to find you. When I told her we don't release teachers' addresses without their permission, she got snippy. Said she has your address but you're not home."

"Give us her description," Dylan said.

"She was tall, slender. Couldn't tell much about her hair or eyes because of her hat and sunglasses."

"How old was she?" Heather asked.

"It was hard to tell. She looked fit and tan, maybe my age—early forties—but she could have been much older."

Dylan quirked an eyebrow. "Why do you say that?"

"Everything about her screamed money—the cut of her beige linen dress, the rocks on her fingers, her Italian shoes. Any woman that loaded could easily afford a face-lift."

Heather attempted to place such a woman and drew a blank. "Did she say anything else, like how I can get in touch with her?"

Darlene shook her head. "She refused, even after I told her I didn't know where you were."

"So she left?" Dylan asked.

Darlene nodded. "She turned on her expensive heels and marched right out to her car."

"Did you get a look at the vehicle?" Dylan persisted.

"It would have been hard to miss. The parking lot's practically empty this time of year, and none of us drives a fancy white Mercedes."

Chapter Nine

"A white Mercedes?" Heather's look of astonishment reflected Dylan's surprise.

"Late model, two-door?" he asked.

"That's right." Darlene sighed with relief. "So you do know her? That's good. She seemed so frantic, I was getting real worried for you, Heather."

As if in shock, Heather didn't comment.

"The address you came for?" Dylan prompted.

Heather blinked, as if coming out of a fog. "I need an address for Kayla Tipton's father."

Darlene's face brightened. "That pretty, dark-haired girl in your senior honors class? I'll only take a minute."

The secretary returned to her desk behind the counter and clicked a few keys on her computer. "The Tiptons live on Shell Island."

Heather jotted the house number and street as Darlene read from the screen.

"Do you have a place of business for the father?" Dylan asked.

Darlene scrolled down the page and produced an address on Beach Drive near the waterfront.

Heather added it to her notes. "Thanks, you've been a big help."

"No problem," Darlene said with a toothy smile. "Say, if that woman comes back, what should I tell her?"

Dylan pulled out his card, wrote his cell phone number and a number for Detective Cramer on the back, and handed it to Darlene. "Try to detain her, and call one of these numbers."

The secretary regarded Heather with a frown. "You're not in some kind of trouble?"

Heather opened her mouth, as if to explain, then shook her head. "Thanks again."

Before the secretary could ask more questions, Dylan steered Heather out of the office and waited until they were out of earshot before speaking. "Think carefully. Is it possible Chip's kidnapper was a woman?"

Confusion clouded her green eyes. "Maybe. He—she could have worn a wig and beard to hide that fact. I can't remember the voice. I was too terrified by the words. A woman athlete or one who weight-trains could have been that strong, but wouldn't the Rowlands have recognized a woman's voice when the kidnapper questioned them this morning?"

"Not necessarily. We had a female dispatcher a few years back with a voice deeper than mine." He opened the Jeep door for her, then circled the vehicle and climbed in.

"Suppose," she said, as he drove away from the school, "the woman in the white Mercedes has nothing to do with the kidnapping or murder attempts?"

"I've heard of stranger coincidences," he admitted, "but if she's not the kidnapper, it's more likely she's connected to him and came to the school either to locate you or to warn you."

"I've never met Mrs. Tipton," Heather said.

"What?" He couldn't follow the leap of Heather's thoughts.

She strained against her seat belt as she turned toward him, and the pressure of the strap across her high, firm breasts generated vivid memories of their earlier embrace. Desire drove all other thoughts from his mind and urged him to stop the car and take her, right there on Fourth Avenue North, in front of God and everybody.

He shoved the air conditioner control to high, aimed the vent at his overheated face and forced himself to concentrate on what Heather was saying.

"Robert Tipton is a very wealthy man. If his wife drives a white Mercedes, maybe he's the man behind this nightmare. If he is, it's almost over."

The eagerness in her voice saddened him. He understood her desire to end the threats against her and Chip, but wondered if she was just as anxious to return to her former life without Dylan. Replaying their conversation at lunch, he recalled her insistence that love was always a risk.

Risk?

He tamped down a snort of disgust. Love was risky all right, and he should know. He'd loved her, and she'd left him. She'd been right about another thing, too. In spite of the pain he'd suffered at her desertion, he wouldn't trade anything for the years they'd spent together.

He turned onto Beach Drive, found the number

Heather read from her notes and parked beneath the canopied shade of a banyan tree. Robert Tipton's law office reeked of affluence, from the lushly landscaped, brick-paved parking lot to the Tiffany-glass panels in the entrance of the converted Victorian mansion.

Plush burgundy runners muffled their footsteps on the polished hardwood floor of the entry hallway, and an elegantly coiffed receptionist raised her head at their approach to her desk.

"May I help you?" Her quiet, genteel voice matched the decor.

Dylan showed his shield. "I'm Officer Dylan Wade of the Dolphin Bay Police Department. I need to speak with Robert Tipton."

If the badge fazed her, she didn't show it. "Have a seat. I'll see if Mr. Tipton is free."

She cast an inquisitive glance at Heather, but Dylan declined to introduce her. He wanted to note Tipton's expression when Heather walked in unannounced.

Heather settled onto a sofa and clasped her hands in her lap. The strain of the past few days had caused violet shadows beneath her eyes and worry lines between her brows, but despite those traces of weariness, her resolute posture and the determined set of her jaw signaled her resistance to despair. A woman of less character would be cowering in fear after all she'd been through, but her irrepressible spirit remained undaunted.

Admiration, love and desire ambushed him, but he thrust the emotions aside. He had a job to do. Then he would get the hell out of her life before wanting her drove him nuts.

"Let me speak to Tipton alone first," he said.

"Okay." Her smile burned through him like sweet acid, a reminder of all he'd lost when she left him.

"Officer Wade." The receptionist had returned. "Mr. Tipton will see you now."

He followed the elegant blonde to the end of the hall. She opened one of the paneled double doors and motioned him inside.

Robert Tipton rose behind a massive mahogany desk set in a bay alcove overlooking a walled garden. In spite of distinguished gray hair and deep lines in his tanned face, his physique and agility matched that of a much younger man. Buttoning the double-breasted jacket of his expensive suit, he stepped from behind his desk with a congenial smile and extended a hand.

"How can I help you, officer?" The attorney's strong grip matched his appearance. He released Dylan's hand and waved him toward a wing chair upholstered in soft burgundy leather. "Coffee?"

"No, thanks." Dylan scanned the room with a practiced eye, taking in photographs in ornate silver frames displayed on a credenza behind Tipton's desk. "Nice family."

"My wife, Catherine." Tipton sat in the matching chair opposite Dylan and pointed to the photo of a tall, slender woman with her arms around a pretty but sulky teenager. "And my daughter, Kayla."

"You're a hunter?" Dylan indicated another picture with Tipton in camouflage clothing, kneeling beside the carcass of a deer in a wooded clearing.

"When I have time," the lawyer said. "I bagged that deer in Minnesota last year."

"With that rifle?" Dylan indicated the weapon Tipton grasped in the photo.

"A Winchester Model 70. It's a great gun."

"With a telescopic sight?"

Tipton stiffened. "Why are you here, Officer Wade?"

"I'm investigating a kidnapping and attempted murder."

"Is one of my clients a suspect?"

"Not that I know of."

The attorney rose from the chair and returned to the seat behind his desk, as if to distance himself from Dylan and his questions. "Who was the subject of this kidnap and murder attempt?"

"Chip Taylor and his mother, Heather."

Tipton's closed expression revealed nothing. "Heather Taylor who teaches at the high school?"

"That's right," Dylan said. "I understand you threatened to destroy her job a few weeks ago."

Tipton's tight smile didn't reach his eyes, and his tone was biting. "As an attorney, I would be remiss to answer any more questions without the benefit of counsel."

"Only if you're guilty." Dislike for the pompous attorney churned in Dylan's gut. "If you can establish alibis for a few critical dates and times, you could save us both a lot of bother."

Tipton punched the button on his intercom. "Ms. Zach, get Walter Fedderson on the phone."

"Let me run a ballistics check on your rifles, and handguns, if you have them," Dylan said. If Tipton was innocent, he probably wouldn't object. "If the slugs used in the shooting don't match those from your guns—"

The attorney interrupted him with a sharp laugh. "I've seen too many innocent people tormented, even convicted, because of overzealous police tactics. If you have any more questions, you'll have to wait until my lawyer arrives."

The phone buzzed on Tipton's desk. He answered, listened without speaking, then hung up. "My attorney is in court. So unless you have a warrant..."

Dylan stood and strode toward the door. At the threshold, he turned. "As I told you, you have a nice family, Mr. Tipton. If anyone ever tries to kidnap your daughter or murder your wife, I hope the police receive more cooperation in their investigation than you've given me."

He stepped into the hall and closed the door behind him. When he reached the reception area, Heather stood. "Do you want me to go in now?"

He shook his head. "It would be a waste of time."

She took long steps to keep up with him as he hurried to his car. "You've crossed him off as a suspect?"

He climbed into the driver's seat and started the Jeep. "It's not that simple. I don't know whether Tipton's refusal to answer questions comes from guilt or legal paranoia."

In the passenger seat beside him, Heather sighed. "So we don't know any more now than we did before."

"I wouldn't say that." He pulled out of the parking lot onto the street. "From the pictures displayed in his office, I know it's possible Mrs. Tipton was the woman at the school, and Tipton owns a rifle with a scope.''

''As you law enforcement types are prone to say, that evidence is only circumstantial.''

He reached for her hand and gave it an encouraging squeeze. ''If the ballistics report on the slug from your pantry indicates the bullet could have come from a Winchester Model 70, that and Tipton's threats against you might be probable cause, enough for a warrant to check Tipton's guns.''

''Are you going to question Mrs. Tipton?''

''He's probably already contacted her with a warning not to speak to anyone without their attorney, and their attorney's still in court.''

She withdrew her hand from his grasp and sat silently for a moment. ''Can we go back to your folks now? I want to see Chip.''

''Sure.'' Frustrated at their lack of success at discovering the kidnapper—and by his own desire, he merged the Jeep into interstate traffic and headed for Dolphin Bay.

HEATHER ROSE FROM the rocker with Chip asleep in her arms and laid him in the crib in the Wades' guest room. Although he had squealed with happiness at her return, his contentment with his grandparents was clear. If anything good had come from the chaos of the past few days, it was Chip's relationship with Margaret and Frank. No little boy could ask for better grandparents.

Earlier, Margaret had insisted Dylan stay for supper. Heather, remembering his embrace earlier that day and hoping to ease her craving for his arms around her, had longed for his departure.

He hadn't cooperated with her unspoken wish for him to leave. He'd remained after the dishes had been cleared, and for the past hour, he and his parents had talked quietly around the kitchen table while Heather prepared Chip for bed.

Although it was still early, she decided to turn in rather than face Dylan and her mutinous yearning again. She had changed into her nightgown when a soft knock sounded on her door.

"Who is it?" she whispered.

"Me," Dylan answered quietly. "Mom and Dad want you to join us in the kitchen."

She leaned against the door, weak from the responsive vibrations his voice had generated. "I'm going to bed."

"There's something we have to discuss. Tonight."

His stern tone alarmed her, but she hesitated. With Margaret and Frank present, however, she was unlikely to succumb to anything as foolish as she had this morning when she'd returned Dylan's kiss. If he hadn't broken away...

"Okay. I'll be there in a minute."

She waited until his footsteps faded down the hall, then tugged on her robe and slippers. After assuring that Chip slept soundly, she followed Dylan into the kitchen and sat at the table across from Frank. Margaret placed a cup of coffee in front of her.

"It's decaf," the older woman said, "so don't worry about it keeping you awake."

Margaret's ordinarily pleasant voice was strained, her smile tenuous, and she avoided Heather's gaze.

Her strange, almost guilty behavior increased Heather's alarm. The warnings clanged louder when Frank, too, avoided her eyes.

A terrifying possibility for the Wades' discomfort occurred to her. Had the low voices she'd heard from her bedroom been plotting to take Chip away from her? Had Dylan convinced his parents to help him gain custody of his son?

She refused to endure another minute of agonizing suspense. "Is there something you want to tell me?"

Frank looked up from his hands, which he'd been studying since she'd first sat at the table. "We want to take Chip—"

"You can't have him." She congratulated herself on her unruffled refusal.

Moving from where he'd leaned against the counter, Dylan stepped behind her and placed his hands on her shoulders. She nearly rose from her seat, but forced herself to listen, as he said, "Don't jump to conclusions. Let Dad finish."

Frank's smile was apologetic. "I guess I phrased that wrong. Maybe I'd better start over."

"Tell her," Margaret encouraged her husband with a nod, "just like we decided."

Distracted by Dylan's warm grip, Heather struggled to concentrate on Frank's explanation.

"We're all worried about your safety, yours and Chip's." Even with his graying hair and aging face, Frank was a handsome man. He looked like Dylan would in thirty years. "Until we can identify who's after you, keeping you safe is iffy business."

"Surely we're safe enough here," she protested. "But if we're a bother—"

"You're no bother." Margaret patted her hand. "We love having you and Chip. But that's not the point."

"The point—" Dylan spoke from behind her and gripped her shoulders tighter "—is that the person we're looking for is clever and determined. Since we don't know whether we're dealing with a man or a woman, the person could have been watching your house, even following us without our knowledge. By now, whoever it is probably knows me and my car."

"And they know you were with Dylan when he interviewed suspects today," Frank added.

The direction of their thinking became suddenly clear. "You think the kidnapper will try to find me through Dylan?"

"It's a logical assumption." Dylan's fingers worked soothing circles against her shoulders, a delicious counterpoint to her tension.

"Dylan and Frank are the only Wades in Dolphin Bay," Margaret said. "Even though neither is listed in the telephone directory, finding our house would be easy for someone determined enough."

Frank cleared his throat. "Jake Emerson, my former partner, has a little house on Crystal River about an hour's drive north. Because it's in Jake's name, and we haven't worked together for years, no one would think to look for you and Chip there."

"You want Chip and me to move to the river?" Imagining the isolation, Heather shuddered.

"You wouldn't be alone," Margaret assured her. "Frank and I would go with you."

Dylan clasped her shoulders again. "I'll stay here to search for the kidnapper."

"No," Heather said.

"No?" He dropped his hands and circled to face her. "Chip's my son, too. I won't let you risk—"

"Now who's jumping to conclusions? It's a good idea for Margaret and Frank to take Chip to the river. But I'm not going."

"Why?" Margaret asked.

"Because I might lead whoever's trying to kill me to Chip. He'll be safer with just the two of you."

"Where will you stay?" Frank asked.

"I'll go home."

"That's crazy." Dylan's angry voice echoed in the quiet house. "Or suicidal."

"I want this nightmare over, and it won't end until we catch the kidnapper."

"How will putting yourself at risk accomplish that?" Compared to her son's, Margaret's tone was gentle.

"If the kidnapper can't find me, he'll simply lay low until I show up again. But if he knows where I am, he's more likely to try something and give us a chance to catch him."

"I won't allow you to risk it," Dylan said.

"Your permission isn't required."

His face flushed with anger. "You have to think of Chip. If anything happened to you—"

The pain in his expression roused her hunger for him. She longed to embrace him and kiss the torment from his face, but concern for her son came first. "I *am* thinking of Chip. He won't be safe until this maniac is caught. If Chip and I both go into hiding, the kidnapper might, too."

Dylan slid into the chair beside her and covered

her hands, gripped on the tabletop until her knuckles paled, with his. "I interviewed two men today, both with hate in their eyes when they spoke of you. Either one could be the man who tried to kill you, who may try again. Please, go to the river, at least until Cramer and I have checked out Hayward and Tipton."

"What if it isn't one of them? What if it's that woman? Can't the police put me under twenty-four-hour surveillance to watch for whoever tries something next?"

"She has a point," Frank admitted.

"Frank Wade," Margaret said hotly, "I won't have my grandson's mother used as a lure for a killer."

"Mom's right," Dylan said. "Besides, Cramer told us how shorthanded they are. Round-the-clock surveillance takes too much manpower."

"Then *you* can protect me."

She spoke before the full implication of her words hit, too late to snatch them back. After the way her traitorous body had responded to his kiss this morning, spending every minute with him would be asking for trouble. She held her breath, hoping he'd refuse.

"If you insist on returning home," he said with quiet intensity, "you can bet I'll stick with you, closer than a burr on a dog."

The intimacy of that analogy left her breathless, but she'd accomplished what she wanted. Chip would be safe at the river with Margaret and Frank, and she could concentrate on flushing out the person who had tried to harm her and her son.

As for her own safety, she had no doubt Dylan would do everything possible to safeguard her, but only because doing so was his job and she was the mother of his son. Recalling his adamant rejection of marriage spared her any illusions about his motives.

"When will you leave?" she asked Margaret and Frank.

"Before dawn tomorrow," Frank said. "Jake's going to follow us to make sure we're not tailed by anyone."

Heather looked to Dylan. "I'd like to go with them, long enough to settle Chip in a new place."

"We'll follow in my car," he said. "You'd better pack for Chip, then get some sleep."

Nervous energy had kept her going, but now fatigue drained her. She rose wearily to her feet and hugged Margaret. "I don't know how to thank you and Frank for all you're doing."

Margaret enfolded her in an embrace. "You're family, and we take care of one another."

Margaret released her to Frank, who wrapped her in a hug that squeezed the breath out of her.

"We'll keep Chip safe and happy," he promised.

Blinking back tears of gratitude, Heather told the older Wades good-night. She didn't dare look at Dylan, afraid in her precarious emotional state she'd say or do something she'd regret.

The heat of his gaze seared her, even after she left the room.

THE SUN WAS SINKING into the Gulf of Mexico when Dylan turned the Jeep onto the highway and headed back toward Dolphin Bay.

"Sure you won't change your mind about staying at the river?"

Heather shook her head. "We've been over this a dozen times. Chip will be safer without me. And he's perfectly happy with your mother."

"Mom had plenty of experience."

"She's a natural with kids. Your dad, too. Chip's really looking forward to fishing with his grandpa tomorrow."

She had left Chip in Margaret's lap in the cozy living room of the river cottage, his blond head cradled against her ample bosom while she sang him silly songs. When Heather kissed him goodbye, he hadn't fussed.

Despite Chip's obvious contentment, she missed him. Except for the hours he'd been at day care and with the Wades, she hadn't been away from him since his birth. They'd never before spent as much as twenty-four hours apart. She smiled, remembering the first months of his life when she'd tiptoed to his crib several times every night to gaze in wonder at the tiny miracle and to assure herself he still breathed.

"I don't think it's safe to return to your house tonight," Dylan said.

"Why not?"

"Too easy for someone to hide in the darkness. I'll take you home in the morning, when I can check the house and grounds in daylight."

"I don't mind sleeping at your folks' one more night."

"Good. We'll stop by my house first to pick up my gear."

Contemplating a night under the same roof with him made her giddy. Since she'd first met him, she had longed to see his face on the pillow beside her when she awoke each morning, hoped for the day when marriage would make that dream come true. Breaking off with him hadn't cured her of that dream, no matter how often she reminded herself of his opposition to marriage and lifelong commitment.

She sighed. Keeping her emotional distance with him sleeping down the hall might prove more difficult than separation from Chip.

"I made some calls while you were showing Chip the river," he said. "Cramer had some interesting news."

She twisted toward him. The afterglow of sunset streamed through the car, illuminating his face with the golden luster of polished bronze. "Does he have a suspect?"

"Not yet. Robert Tipton's lawyer called him this morning."

She grimaced. "To complain about your visit?"

"Surprisingly, no. He said the police could pick up his client's guns and run their ballistics checks. The lawyer insists Tipton has nothing to hide."

"Does that mean we can scratch Tipton as a suspect?"

"Not yet. He's too savvy to invite police to check out a rifle he used in a crime, and if he's our shooter, he's had time to dispose of the weapon."

"Looks like we're back where we started."

"Not entirely. According to ballistics, the slug taken from your pantry was either .308 or 30-06 caliber, which would fit either Tipton's or Hayward's rifles. Cramer has a detective verifying Andy Hayward's shooting range alibi. If Hayward lied about his whereabouts, Cramer will have cause to request a warrant to seize his guns for ballistics tests.''

"And those will tell you if Andy was the shooter?''

He nodded. "*If* the rifling in the barrel of one of his guns matches the markings on the slugs.''

Obtaining a warrant and more ballistics tests would take days. She clamped her jaw tight in frustration. Until whoever had kidnapped Chip and tried to kill her was behind bars, her life would remain in limbo. Watching the stars come out as darkness suppressed the lingering colors of the sunset, she settled into her seat and wondered how many more days of this torture she could stand.

Forty-five minutes later, Dylan turned the Jeep into the driveway of his house and shut off the engine. "Have you told your folks about the kidnapping?''

She shook her head. "I didn't want to worry them.'' She glanced at her watch. "I should ring them now, in case they've tried to call me at home. May I use your phone?''

"Come inside. You can call while I get my kit.''

She opened the door, climbed out and paused to stretch muscles tightened by the long drive. Something rustled in the hedge beside the driveway, and she glanced up.

A dark figure hurtled out of the darkness.

A metal blade glimmered in the weak light, and her scream ripped the night air.

Chapter Ten

"Drop the knife!" Gun drawn, Dylan lunged around the Jeep's hood.

Heather, struggling with the masked attacker, blocked Dylan's line of fire. The abrupt termination of her scream as the knife found its mark struck Dylan like a blow to the gut. She crumpled to the ground. Her assailant, using her as a shield, dragged her toward a hedge, then disappeared in the shadows.

Dylan rushed to her and cradled her in his arms. The sticky wetness soaking his shirt and the coppery smell of blood confirmed his fear.

"I'm okay," she said weakly. "Go after him."

Ignoring her protests, he lifted her into the Jeep, fastened her seat belt and slammed the door. As he scurried to the driver's seat, anger choked him—anger at the cold-blooded assassin who had struck down an innocent, unarmed woman. And anger at himself for being caught off guard.

He rammed the Jeep into reverse, lurched out of the drive and peeled down the street in a stench of burning rubber. Erotic fantasies of spending the night with Heather had distracted him, blunted his instincts, lowered his alertness. He should have been vigilant, on guard for trouble even before he stopped the Jeep.

With tires squealing, he rounded the corner, one hand on the wheel, the other on his phone. Thankful he'd programmed the PD with a one-digit code, he placed an instant call to the station.

Sandi, the dispatcher, answered.

"Send Tom Mackey to my house," Dylan said, "and request a K-9 unit. Someone attacked Heather with a knife, then took off on foot through the backyard."

"Stand by."

Sandi's steady voice, dispatching Mackey and backup to Dylan's address, carried through the open line. Mackey must have been close by, because the sound of sirens erupted only a few blocks away.

"Do you need an ambulance?" Sandi asked when she returned to the phone.

"Negative. I'm driving Heather to the emergency room now."

"I'll send an officer for a statement as soon as one's free."

Dylan tossed the phone onto the dashboard and reached for Heather. Her forehead was cold and clammy beneath his hand, and trembling racked her body. Praying she wasn't going into shock, he pressed harder on the accelerator.

"It's just a scratch." He could barely hear her weak murmur above the whine of the racing engine. "Maybe you'd better slow down."

The tightness in her voice and her hiss of indrawn breath contradicted her words. A scratch didn't cause that kind of pain or that much bleeding. He grabbed her hand to reassure her and had to squelch his panic at the slick dampness sliding down her arm.

"We're almost there." He dug a handkerchief from his pocket and passed it to her. "Apply pressure to the wound. You have to stop the bleeding."

"I'll try."

If her hands were as weak as her voice, she couldn't do much good. Intent on getting her medical care as soon as possible, he hadn't taken time to evaluate her injury. If the attacker had struck an artery or vital organ...

He leaned toward her, driving with his left hand while his right compressed the handkerchief she'd placed over her left forearm.

"Is that your only wound?" he asked.

"Yes." Her voice had faded further. "Sorry I'm being such a baby. It's just a little cut."

When the man attacked, she had raised her arm to protect herself, and it had taken the full force of his knife. Imagining the pain and picturing the damage, the blood she'd lost, Dylan winced.

Suddenly, her words from yesterday rang in his mind: *Loving is always a risk, because, sooner or later, we're all terminal.*

Warm wetness oozed between his fingers, which squeezed the handkerchief against her arm, stanching the blood and preventing her life from draining out of her.

Not yet, he prayed, silently and furiously. *You can't have her yet. Chip needs her. I need her.*

His admission shocked him. He'd spent the past two years convincing himself how well he could manage without her. What a damned fool he'd been. Heather was so much a part of him, he might as well try not breathing as not loving her. He didn't want to muddle through life without her. He wanted her with him—forever.

Arrival at the emergency entrance interrupted his self-condemnation. He slid his arms beneath her and lifted her from the car. Although he could see her teeth gritted in pain, she forced a feeble smile. The stark white of her skin contrasted with the glittering green of her eyes for only seconds before her eyelids fluttered and closed.

Hugging her against his chest, he raced inside, yelling for a doctor.

As part of his job, he had spent more time in the emergency room than he cared to remember, and that familiarity served him well now. Orderlies and nurses, recognizing the Dolphin Bay police officer, hurried to Heather's assistance.

Gentle hands pried her from him, shifted her to a gurney and rolled her down the tiled passageway. Other hands pressed him into a seat in the hall and supplied him with a cup of steaming coffee.

In a daze, he completed Heather's admission form, then slumped in his chair and leaned his head against the wall. The odor of antiseptic bit his nostrils, triggering a flood of vivid memories.

He had sat in this same corridor the night Clyde Heller had been shot, and he'd never forget Annie's face when she rushed through the double glass doors, looking as if her whole world had collapsed on top of her. At the time, he'd believed he understood how she felt, but he hadn't.

He understood now.

Fear for Heather, fear of losing her forever, gnawed at him, and the possibility of a future without her opened before him like a cold, black abyss.

He set aside his empty coffee cup, ran his fingers through his hair and struggled against the helplessness that gripped him. Heather had been right about loving and risking. He had always loved her but had refused to gamble on commitment, fearful that the stresses and uncertainties of his job would drive a severing wedge between them.

Now he'd give anything for a chance at marriage. If Heather recovered—*when* she recovered—he wanted to be a husband to her and a father to Chip.

Irony stung him. He'd come too late to his decision. She had decided two years ago she didn't love him, didn't want his help raising their child, and, for the life of him, he couldn't figure how or why her love for him had died.

Stirring hope nudged his irony aside. When he'd kissed her yesterday, he had felt her need, as great as his own. Maybe, if she pulled through, he could douse the anger he'd glimpsed scudding over her face like a fast-moving cloud and rekindle the love that had once shone there.

Closing his eyes, he prayed, trying not to think of the last time he'd pleaded with God. His prayers for Clyde Heller had gone unanswered.

An eternity and five cups of bad coffee later, Dr. Jarrett, the emergency room physician who had treated several crime and accident victims Dylan had escorted to the hospital, advanced up the hall from where Heather had been taken.

Fear seized Dylan's lungs like a vise, cutting off his air. In bloodstained scrubs, the ER doctor, slack-jawed, with dull eyes and somber countenance, looked like the bearer of bad news. Only when Jarrett's weary face broke into a smile was Dylan able to breathe again. "How is she?"

"She's in the recovery room now. We've had her in surgery to repair the ulnar artery so she won't lose the use of her hand. I don't think there's any permanent damage."

"When can I take her home?"

"I'd like to keep her overnight for observation. Although the damage could have been fatal if unrepaired, the surgical procedure was relatively minor. She can probably be discharged tomorrow."

"Can I see her?"

Jarrett shook his head. "She's still—"

"Please."

Jarrett's eyes narrowed. "She can't be questioned now."

"I'm not here as a police officer. I'm..." Dylan searched for words to explain their ambiguous relationship and silently cursed his ineptitude. "She's..."

"She must be special," Jarrett said with an understanding smile. "We'll take her up to a room on the surgery floor soon. Once she's settled, a few minutes' visit won't hurt, but don't wake her if she's sleeping."

Dylan paced the hall for another eternity until a gray-haired nurse approached. "You can go up now, Officer Wade. Ms. Taylor is in Room 434."

He sprinted to the elevator, cursed its lack of speed

and exited onto the fourth floor. He raced down the hall and forced himself to slow at the door to her room before stepping inside.

As white as her pillowcase, Heather lay unconscious, her sun-bleached chestnut hair a stark contrast to her pallor. Her slender body, a slight mound beneath the hospital blanket and a visible reminder of how fragile she was, barely moved with her breathing.

He circled the bed to avoid the apparatus transfusing fluids into her right arm and took care not to jostle her bandaged left forearm. Brushing a curl from her forehead, he placed a gentle kiss on her cool brow, then touched his lips to hers. Eyes closed, she stirred briefly, and her lips lifted in a ghost of a smile.

Overpowering love and a tender protectiveness welled inside him. He had so much he wanted to say to her, but he struggled to find the words. A discreet cough behind him interrupted his effort.

Reluctantly, he straightened. Tom Mackey's uniformed bulk filled the doorway. After a quick glance at the slumbering Heather, Dylan retreated from the room to join the officer in the hall.

"Any luck?" Dylan asked.

Mackey frowned. "We brought in the K-9, but the dog lost the scent on the next block. The perp must have parked his car there for a quick getaway. I put out an APB for a white Mercedes—"

"Add a black sport utility vehicle."

"Did you see it?"

Dylan shook his head. "Whoever's been stalking Heather has been seen driving one or the other of those vehicles. The attacker could be in either to-night.''

Mackey pulled a notebook from his shirt pocket and jotted a few words. ''Did you get a good look at him?''

''Average height—for a man. An inch or two taller than Heather. Black shirt and pants, black watch cap over the face with cutouts for the eyes.''

''Build?''

Dylan thought hard, pulling up the image from memory. ''Not bulked up like a weight lifter. Possibly slender. The loose clothing made it hard to tell.''

Mackey paused, pencil poised. ''It *was* a man?''

''Or a tall woman in men's clothing.''

Mackey scratched his head and frowned. ''You just doubled the number of possible suspects.''

''I wish I could be more specific. Whoever it was is fast on his feet.''

''Did you see the weapon?''

''A standard butcher knife, the kind you'd find in any kitchen in town.''

Mackey scribbled some more. ''The crime scene unit is scouring the area. Maybe the guy dropped it.''

''Finding it probably won't help much. The attacker wore gloves. This one's too clever to leave prints.''

''Did you fire at him?''

Dylan scowled. ''Heather was between us, so I couldn't get a clear shot. Why?''

Mackey shuffled his feet and avoided Dylan's eyes. ''There was lots of blood at the scene, I thought maybe... How's Heather?''

A lump formed in Dylan's throat at the concern in Mackey's voice. Tom, along with everyone else in the department, had attended cookouts at Dylan's in the days when Heather had been there. The guys had teased her about Dylan, had liked and accepted her.

They also had deliberately avoided mentioning her name when she'd disappeared from his life. Tonight every last one of them would be busting his butt, tracking the man—or woman—who had tried to kill her. The men on the force were a tightly knit bunch, like family. If someone messed with one of them or their loved ones, he'd messed with them all and should be prepared for the consequences.

Dylan cleared the emotion from his throat. "Dr. Jarrett says she'll be okay, but he's keeping her overnight. I'll stand guard."

Mackey contemplated him with a measuring eye. "You look whipped. You should go home and sleep."

"I can't. That creep's still out there—"

"I'll find one of the guys to relieve you." Mackey flashed a consoling grin and clapped him on the shoulder. "This is one helluva vacation you're taking, bud."

Mackey strode toward the elevator, and Dylan tiptoed into Heather's room to assure himself she still slept soundly. Returning to the corridor, he used his cell phone to leave a message on Cramer's beeper.

Minutes later, he settled into the chair beside Heather's bed and waited. When Cramer called, Dylan would give him a full report. To keep Heather safe, he would need all the help he could get.

MURMURING VOICES and muted footsteps pierced Heather's consciousness, light filtered through her closed lids, and her mouth, dry as cobwebs, craved water. Pain sizzled down her left arm as if someone had branded it with a hot poker.

She opened her eyes to a white ceiling and unfamiliar sea-foam-green walls. Through a wide window to her left, the calm waters of Dolphin Bay glimmered like mother-of-pearl beneath the rising sun.

She remembered climbing out of the Jeep and the flash of a knife in the dark. Everything afterward was either a blur or a blank.

Dropping her gaze to the bandages on her forearm, she focused on the pain. Someone had attacked her.

Where was Dylan?

Anxiety gripped her. Had he been hurt, too?

Turning her head on the pillow, she saw him.

Slumped in a chair beside her bed, head resting on arms folded atop her blanket, he slept. Fine dark hair tumbled over his forehead, long lashes fanned against tanned skin, and he frowned, as if he were dreaming.

Too groggy to move or speak, she studied his profile, an older version of Chip's, and savored the latent power of his shoulders and his strong, capable hands.

Memories of the previous night unsettled her. Blocking out details of the terrifying attack, she concentrated on the aftermath. She was lucky Dylan had been there. Even during the first year they were together, his reputation for coolheadedness under pressure was already legendary.

At one weekend party after an especially harrowing work week, Larry Shelton had raised his glass in a toast. "To Dylan, the best guy to have around in a crisis."

Fifteen men and their wives, many with tears in their eyes, had joined in the tribute. Earlier that week, a woman whose four-year-old had fallen into a swimming pool had flagged down Dylan on his routine patrol. He'd leaped from his cruiser, dived into the deep water for the child and administered CPR until the paramedics arrived. The little girl had lived.

Displaying that same imperturbable calm, he'd saved her life last night by stanching the flow of her blood and rushing her to the emergency room. Judging from the shadowy stubble on his face and the clothes he'd worn the day before, he hadn't left the hospital since her admittance.

She had believed her love already so immense that she couldn't love him more, but she'd been wrong. The pleasing ache of overpowering affection surged in her veins, overshadowing the pain in her arm. She raised her hand to caress his hair.

A needle, connected to intravenous tubing, pinched her arm, a reminder of how close she'd come to dying in spite of Dylan's help. Cold fear, not for herself, but for Chip, washed through her. If she had died, what would have happened to her son?

Dylan lifted his head. The sweetness of his slowly spreading smile poured through her like a balm, calming her fears.

He considered her, his dark eyes heavy with sleep. "Good morning."

She returned his smile. Waking up to Dylan could be habit-forming.

When he cupped her cheek with his hand, worry shadowed his eyes. "How are you feeling?"

She wobbled her hand in a so-so gesture and tried to speak, but her dry mouth refused to cooperate. She managed only one word. "Chip?"

"I called Mom and Dad." Dylan stood and stretched, muscles rippling beneath his shirt. "Chip's as happy as a pig in mud. Jake Emerson and his wife drove to the river cottage earlier this morning. He and Dad will take turns standing guard, just in case."

She nodded and licked her parched lips. Noting her thirst, Dylan sat beside her, put an arm around her to help her sit up, and held the straw from a tumbler of cold water to her lips. In the comforting haven of his embrace, she drank greedily.

"Not too much. You may be queasy from the anesthetic."

The water restored her speech. "I had surgery?"

"To repair the artery in your arm." He set aside the glass but continued to hold her.

She snuggled deeper into the warm circle of his arms. "Did they catch the man who knifed me?"

His muscles tensed. "The full shift and most of the guys off duty are looking for him now. So far, it's as if he disappeared into thin air."

Heather shivered. The public hospital with its staff, visitors and countless entrances and exits seemed suddenly less secure. The attack last night had caught both her and Dylan by surprise. Here, confined to bed, with no idea what her assailant looked like, not knowing if a male or female stalked her, she presented an easy and accessible target.

"Don't worry." Dylan tightened his arms around

her. "I promise I won't let him near you again. And this time, I have help."

He nodded toward the open door. A uniformed officer with his back to her room watched the hallway. Although she couldn't see his face, his alert stance and the Dolphin Bay Police Department patch on his sleeve eased her immediate fears.

But she couldn't shake her nagging anxiety.

She and Chip couldn't return home until the stalker was behind bars, and the longer she remained with Dylan, the harder leaving him again would be. Weariness and the ache in her arm sapped her energy, leaving her too exhausted to cope with her dilemma.

"What am I going to do?" Her groggy murmur sounded as if someone else was speaking.

"You're going to sleep. Jeb Greenlea's standing guard in the hall, and I'm staying right here." Dylan shifted her gently onto the pillow, smoothed her covers and lowered his lips to hers.

She wanted to tell him he needed rest, too, but her mouth refused to cooperate. Savoring the taste of his kiss, she drifted into unconsciousness.

THE PRESSURE OF A HAND on his shoulder roused Dylan from a deep sleep. Instantly alert and reaching for his gun, he leaped from his chair.

"Easy, Wade. It's me, Cramer."

Dylan's vision focused, and when he recognized the St. Pete detective, he relaxed. "What are you doing here?"

"Have you made an arrest?" Heather asked from her bed.

"No." Cramer waved Dylan back into his seat. "But we've made some progress, of sorts."

Still punchy from sleep, Dylan sank into his chair. Heather pushed the bed's remote control and raised herself to a sitting position. Her color had returned, and when she'd spoken, her voice was stronger. Dylan uttered a silent prayer of gratitude, then turned his attention to Cramer. "What kind of progress?"

Cramer perched on the wide windowsill, removed his glasses and began cleaning the lenses with his tie. "We've eliminated two suspects."

"Who?" Surprise drove the last dregs of sleep from Dylan's mind.

"The range officer backed up Andy Hayward's alibi." Cramer held his glasses to the light to check for spots. "Andy was target shooting every morning, just like he said."

"So he couldn't have kidnapped Chip or shot at me," Heather said.

"Yeah, and the guy obviously doesn't have the money to pay someone else to do his dirty work," Dylan observed.

Cramer jammed his glasses on. "Tipton's alibi checks out, too. We questioned his wife, asked if she tried to reach Ms. Taylor at her school, but Ms. Tipton was out of town, with witnesses to vouch for her."

"And Tipton's guns?" Dylan asked.

"He insisted we run a ballistics check on every one. None of the slugs from his rifles matched the ones taken from Ms. Taylor's kitchen."

"And the pistols?"

"No matches with the markings on the cartridges from the packing house."

Heather looked thoughtful. "Unlike Andy, Robert Tipton *does* have the money to pay someone else to kidnap Chip or shoot at me."

"But what's his motive?" Cramer said. "I interviewed several of his friends. The guy was hot when his daughter didn't make valedictorian, but he got over it."

"Anything on the others on Heather's list?" Dylan asked.

"We've questioned them all, but none is a likely suspect. Most had alibis. A few didn't know who Ms. Taylor is."

"They could be lying," Dylan said.

"True," Cramer said, "but my men are good. They know the subtle signals to watch for."

"*Somebody's* trying to kill her. That knife wound isn't a figment of her imagination."

Behind his thick lenses, Cramer considered Heather with gloomy eyes. "I'm sorry, Ms. Taylor. I wish we could catch the son of a…gun, but our investigation has hit a wall. Unless there's something you haven't told us?"

She shook her head. "Nobody wants this ended more than I do. If I could think of anything—"

"I'm sure you'll let me know." Cramer rose from the windowsill and smoothed his crumpled tie. "Take care of that arm. Wade, keep me informed."

When Cramer left, Dylan turned to Heather. The afternoon sun streaming in the window lit her face with an ethereal glow. Remembering how close she'd come to becoming the angel she resembled, he suppressed a chill. "You're looking better."

"I'm feeling well enough to leave." Her brief smile melted his insides. With her good hand, she began rummaging through the drawers of the bedside table and rolling tray.

"What are you doing?"

"Looking for pencil and paper."

"Why?"

"To make a plan."

An inveterate listmaker and organizer, Heather had always approached every challenge with a blueprint. Loss of blood and an armful of sutures apparently hadn't dissuaded her. He didn't try to stop her search. Might as well attempt to halt the tide. "A plan? What for?"

She located a piece of hospital stationery and a ballpoint pen. Pulling the tray across her lap, she wrote *plan* in block letters across the top of the paper. "To catch the stalker."

"You don't catch a stalker with a plan. You need clues, motives, witnesses—"

"Been there, done that, and it got us nowhere. No, actually, I ended up here. So *now* we'll make a plan."

Her eyes glittered like emeralds flecked with gold. Afraid she might be feverish, he placed his wrist to her forehead. It felt cool against his skin.

She slapped his hand away. "We'll never get anything done if you don't cooperate."

Lovemaking, not cooperation, was what he had in mind, but the hospital room was neither the time nor place.

Resigned to allowing her organizational impulse to run its course and prepared to humor her, he sank into the chair. "What kind of plan do you have in mind?"

"A trap."

He didn't like the direction she was headed.

She put down her pen and leaned toward him. "When has this stalker shown himself?"

In spite of his intentions to accommodate her, he sighed. "We've been through all this before. What's the point?"

Her brief flare of animation ended, and her expression turned grim. "This person has appeared four times. First when he kidnapped Chip, at the ransom drop, when he shot up my kitchen and, finally, last night. The one common factor on all four occasions is me."

"Wait a minute. You're not—"

"Yes, I am. I intend to be the bait in the trap we set."

"That's crazy. You were almost killed—"

"We were both caught by surprise. We won't let that happen again."

He swallowed a gulletful of guilt. *He* shouldn't have been surprised by the attack. He should have been vigilant. She owed her survival, not to him, but to the proximity of Dolphin Bay Memorial Hospital and the skill of its staff. If she had died, her death would have been on his conscience.

"No, putting you in harm's way is too risky."

She shoved the fingers of her right hand through her hair and glared at him. "What's *your* plan?"

"We'll wait for another lead—"

"Or another attack? Don't you see?" Her voice softened. "I'm the bait, whether we have a plan or not."

Chapter Eleven

However much Dylan hated the circumstances that put Heather at risk, he knew she was right. She was the killer's prime target, whether Dylan wanted her to be or not.

"Chip and I can't hide forever," she said. "We want our lives back."

Ask her, an inner voice taunted, *ask her if one reason she's so anxious to have her life back is to get rid of you.*

But he couldn't form the question. He was too afraid of the answer.

"We'll make a plan," he conceded, "but we'll do it my way. First—"

A rap sounded at the door, and Dr. Jarrett entered the room. Unlike the previous night, he walked with a bounce to his step and his clothes were wrinkle-free and unbloodied.

"How's my patient?"

Dylan introduced him to Heather, who'd been either anesthetized or asleep in Jarrett's presence until now.

"I'm doing well," she said, "thanks to you."

"And thanks to Dylan. If he hadn't rushed you here so quickly... Anyway, the nurses have given you a good report, although one or two did ask what crime you committed."

"What?"

Dylan laughed. "Patients kept under police protection here are usually ones who've been arrested."

Jarrett removed her bandage, checked her sutures and observed carefully as she flexed her fingers. "Mobility's good, but the incision will be sore for a few days. I'll prescribe some painkillers."

"When can I leave?" she asked after he'd applied a fresh bandage.

The doctor cocked his head and considered her. "That depends."

"On what?" Dylan asked.

"On whether there's anyone at home to take care of you. I don't want you using that arm for a few days."

"She's coming home with me," Dylan said. "I'll take care of her."

"In that case," Jarrett said with a good-natured grin, "you're discharged now, Ms. Taylor. I'll tell the nurse to send for a wheelchair."

"What about my clothes?"

Jarrett frowned. "They had to be cut off last night, but you're welcome to the gown you're wearing. I'll have a nurse bring you a robe and slippers, too. And I want to see you in my office next week, sooner if you have a problem."

Dylan followed Jarrett into the hall and, as the doctor moved on to the nurses' station, approached Jeb Greenlea, still on guard.

"Heather's being discharged. I'm taking her to my house."

"I'll follow in the cruiser. Detective Sergeant Bullock said to keep her under close watch."

"Good idea."

At the end of the hall, the elevator doors opened, and Dylan tensed, instantly alert. When a teenage volunteer in a pink-and-white-striped uniform rolled an empty wheelchair onto the floor, he relaxed again.

The girl's freckled face lit up when she saw him. "Hi, Dylan."

He recognized the daughter of his mother's neighbor. "Hello, Cindy. This way."

Cindy pushed the wheelchair into Heather's room, and he followed. While Cindy chattered nonstop about the movie she'd seen the night before, a nurse bustled in and helped Heather into a hospital robe, disposable slippers and a sling for her bandaged arm.

After Heather was dressed, he and the nurse supported her on either side and installed her in the wheelchair that Cindy held immobile.

"All set?" he asked Heather.

The effort of moving from the bed to the chair had sapped her strength, but not her spirit. She nodded with a dazzling smile.

The nurse left, Cindy gripped the wheelchair to push it forward, and Heather bent over her arm to adjust her sling.

"Wow," Cindy said suddenly. "Are you related to Mrs. Sinclair?"

"Rand Sinclair's wife?" Dylan asked.

"Yeah, that's the one."

Heather met his gaze with a puzzled look. "We're

not related. I've never met her, but I know her husband.''

His instincts prickled. "Why do you ask?"

Cindy pointed to the back of Heather's neck. "When she bent over, I saw the mark, right at her hairline.''

He circled the chair, lifted the hair off Heather's neck and observed the tiny birthmark in the shape of an almost perfect heart, a spot he had kissed more than once. "You mean this?"

Cindy nodded.

"I've had that all my life," Heather said to the girl. "What's the big deal?"

"It's just a weird coincidence," Cindy said with a shrug. "About an hour ago, Mrs. Sinclair was released from the maternity ward. The doctor said her labor pains were false, so he sent her home.''

"What's Jasmine Sinclair got to do with Heather?" he insisted.

Cindy shrugged again. "Probably nothing, except she has the exact same mark in the exact same place. What are the odds of that?"

Pretty long odds—unless they're related.

The solution, unexpected and out of the blue, almost knocked him off his feet. Glad he was standing behind Heather so she couldn't witness the shock on his face, he said nothing.

He wouldn't voice his conclusions until he'd had time to think them through, but he was convinced the little candy striper had just handed him the key to finding out who was stalking Heather—and why.

DYLAN TOOK HEATHER to his house. His parents' home was big and rambling with too many doors and windows a determined intruder could readily jimmy. At his own much smaller and more secure place, Heather would always be only a few steps away, and he could keep an eye on her more easily.

The next morning after a late breakfast, Dylan waited until Heather was settled in the recliner in his living room before breaking his news. "I have a surprise."

"You're spoiling me. You shouldn't have given up your bed last night. I could have slept on your sofa."

"You need your rest."

"So do you, and you probably didn't get it. I was surprised to wake up and find you sleeping on the floor beside the bed. You'd said you'd take the sofa."

Reluctant to reveal the agony of sleeping so close without her in his arms, he shrugged. "I wanted to be nearby, in case you needed something."

"I'm already much better. Another day or so, and I can toss this sling." Her glow of healthy color confirmed her claim. "Now, what's your surprise?"

Her open and trusting expression stabbed him with fresh doubts. If his instincts were wrong, an awful lot of people were going to be upset for nothing.

"I phoned your folks yesterday afternoon while you were sleeping and told them everything that's happened, from Chip's kidnapping to now."

"You shouldn't have! They'll be worried sick, especially Mom. She's such an alarmist, even over little things. And Dad's heart—"

"That's why I invited them to come see for themselves that you're okay.'' He wouldn't divulge his real motive. Not yet. ''They'll arrive around lunchtime.''

''But they could be in danger here.''

He sank onto the sofa and clasped his hands between his knees. He didn't want to frighten her, but she had a right to know the facts. ''Your parents have already received some strange phone calls.''

''Threats?''

''Inquiries, asking where to find you.''

''Was the caller male or female?''

''Two different callers. One a man's voice, the other a woman's. Both called several times.''

''I suppose it's too much to hope that they identified themselves?''

''Said they were friends of yours from college, trying to contact you about a reunion.''

Her tension eased visibly. ''My five-year reunion *is* this summer, so maybe the calls were a coincidence.''

He shook his head. ''The university gave me the name of the reunion committee chairman. She says they haven't begun calling yet.''

Heather's shocked silence lasted only seconds. ''What did my parents tell these callers?''

''What could they say? Until last night, they didn't know you weren't staying at home, so your dad told them to try you there.''

''A man and a woman,'' she said with a contemplative frown. ''That means *two* people are after me.''

''Maybe. One could be paying the other to make

inquiries. And we can't rule out the possibility of one person disguising both appearance and voice."

She looked so vulnerable and fragile, engulfed in his huge chair, her arm swathed in bandages, that he wanted to sweep her up and carry her far away from danger or worry. But they had nowhere to run, nowhere to hide, especially when they didn't know who was stalking her or why.

He didn't know, but he had an idea.

A glance at his watch prompted him to hurry. If he wanted to give her time to consider his suspicion before her folks arrived, he couldn't delay any longer.

Lifting his head, he met her gaze straight on. "Do you remember Cindy?"

"The little candy striper who pushed my wheelchair yesterday?"

He nodded. "Remember what she said?"

"Not everything," she said with a rueful smile. "She talked a mile a minute. Something about Rand's wife. I didn't even know he was married."

"Jasmine and Rand married last October. I was best man at their wedding."

She grew quiet, obviously reluctant to discuss marriage or weddings. He pushed to his feet and crossed to the front window. Down the street in a dilapidated old Plymouth, Detective Sergeant Sid Bullock slumped in the front seat, keeping Dylan's place under surveillance in hopes the attacker would make another move.

Dylan turned from the window and shoved his hands in his back pockets. "You and Jasmine have a lot in common."

"You mean my birthmark?" She touched the back of her neck. "That's some coincidence, huh?"

He crushed memories of his lips against the nape of her neck. "There's more."

"More?"

"Last September, someone tried to kill Jasmine." He had her complete attention now and could almost see wheels turning in her mind.

"Rand told you about it?"

He nodded. "And I worked on the case."

"Maybe you'd better tell me what happened." Her smile had disappeared.

"Someone burned down Jasmine's house. She barely escaped with her life."

Heather cradled her bandaged arm in her good one, as if remembering the attempt on her own life. "Did they catch who did it?"

"Rand and Jasmine figured it out. Charles Wilcox, the attorney for Sinclair and Moore Construction, wanted Jasmine dead."

"Why?"

"To cover up his earlier crime. Talbot Moore—"

"Rand's guardian?"

He nodded. "Over thirty years ago, Talbot and Lily Ross, Jasmine's mother, fell in love. Charles's sister Irene was also in love with Talbot. To get rid of his sister's rival, Charles abducted Lily and imprisoned her in a psychiatric hospital."

"That's terrible! Charles's love for his sister must be really twisted."

He grimaced. "What Charles loved was Talbot's money."

She wrinkled her nose with its appealing sprinkle

of freckles. "If Talbot married Irene and Lily was hidden away, how did they manage to conceive Jasmine?"

"Years before the abduction, unknown to Talbot, Lily had given birth to their daughter."

"This is more complicated than a soap opera. Why didn't Talbot marry Lily in the first place?"

"When Lily discovered she was pregnant, she didn't tell Talbot." He paused, considering the parallels in the story. Heather hadn't told him about her pregnancy, either. "In fact, Lily refused to see Talbot again, because Charles warned her that marriage to her would ruin Talbot, financially and socially."

"And Lily believed him?"

"Charles Wilcox can be a very charming and persuasive man. He was also supposedly Talbot's best friend, so Lily, not knowing Charles wanted Talbot to marry Irene, believed him."

"If Lily had already backed out of Talbot's life, why did Charles kidnap her?"

"Because she popped in again. When Jasmine was three, Lily's sister became seriously ill. Lily had to quit her job to care for her, so she had no money. She wrote to Talbot, asking for a loan until she could return to work. When Talbot didn't answer, Lily came to Dolphin Bay to see him."

"Had he already married Irene?"

"No, he was still in love with Lily and elated when she appeared unexpectedly at his house. Charles, aware of her arrival, abducted Lily almost immediately, and Talbot never saw her again, until last year."

"How did he find her?"

"Twenty-five years later, Lily's letter, lost all that time, was returned to Jasmine. Only then did Jasmine learn who her father was. Together with Rand, they rescued her mother."

"So Charles tried to kill Jasmine *before* she identified herself as Talbot's daughter?"

He nodded. "Charles didn't want another heir to the family fortune. Now he'll spend the rest of his life in jail."

"What happened to Irene?"

"She married Talbot after Lily disappeared. They had three sons, but their marriage was shaky from the start. Last year, after Lily was set free, Irene and Talbot divorced. She and her youngest son Blain moved to France. Her older sons, T.J. and Art, stayed here to work in their father's company."

"And Lily?"

"Lily and Talbot married a few months ago."

"That's an incredible story." Heather cast him a puzzled glance. "But aside from the attempt on her life and a similar birthmark, I don't see what Jasmine and I have in common."

"Maybe nothing."

She impaled him with a stare. "I know that tone, Dylan Wade. What haven't you told me?"

"The rest of the story."

He'd come to the crux of his tale, and he suddenly lost his nerve. If his hunch was right, what he was about to tell her would turn her world upside down.

"How about a cup of tea?" he asked.

She shook her head. "I want to hear how it ends."

"You may not like it."

"Why not?"

"You're a creature of habit. You don't like change."

"Don't be silly. How can a story change me? Tell me the rest."

Like a diver plunging into deep water, he drew a deep breath and continued. "During the brief time Lily spent with Talbot before Charles kidnapped her, she became pregnant. Once hospitalized, she was constantly sedated to prevent her escape. She has no memory of giving birth or of her baby being taken away."

"How awful." Her eyes misted.

"A few weeks ago, a few of the baby's clothes Lily had stashed away in a lucid moment were forwarded to Moore House by a former nurse. That's how Lily learned about her other child."

As if uncomfortable, Heather shifted in her chair.

"Is your arm bothering you? I can bring you a pain pill."

She shook her head. "Charles told them where to find the missing kid, right?"

"He claims to know nothing. Talbot and Lily can't find any record of the adoption, nothing to indicate the baby even existed."

"Maybe the nurse made the whole thing up and there *was* no baby." Her voice and eyes were peculiarly bright.

He'd always known Heather was a quick study. She'd guessed where he was headed and offered an alternative, as if hoping to avoid his conclusion.

"A note about the baby in Lily's handwriting was with the baby clothes."

With her bottom lip caught in her teeth and her

hand plucking at nonexistent threads on her bandage, she lowered her head, avoiding his eyes. His heart ached for her, and he silently cursed the circumstances that had forced this conversation.

"When your folks arrive, we'll have some answers."

The stubborn tilt of her head and the defensiveness in her voice announced her resistance to his conclusions. "What kind of answers?"

To break through her denial, he'd have to be blunt. "Whether they adopted you."

She flinched as if he'd struck her. "That's impossible. They would never have hidden that fact from me."

"I believe you are Talbot and Lily's missing daughter."

"No!"

Her anguished cry tore at his gut, and he hated the pain he'd caused her, but he'd hate himself more if the next attempt on her life succeeded. He couldn't shield her from the possibility that she had been adopted, not when knowing the truth might save her life.

"Talbot's daughter stands to inherit one-fifth of a tremendous fortune."

Using her one good arm, she struggled to her feet. Her face twisted with anger and heartache. "I don't *care* about Talbot's money—"

"Someone else obviously does."

"What do you mean?"

"Money is a prime motive for murder."

Chapter Twelve

She refused to believe she'd been adopted.

The possibility blew her world apart. The floor dipped, the room spun, and she flung her good arm around Dylan's neck to keep from falling. Pulling her to him, careful of her injury, but hard enough to jolt the air from her lungs, he wrapped his arms around her.

Cold with shock, she clung to him, welcoming his comforting heat, as drawn by his compassion as she was repelled by his adoption theory.

Tears stung her eyes, and she choked back a sob. "My parents—"

"They'll always be your parents." His breath fanned her cheek. "Nothing changes the love and care they've given you all your life."

"Why didn't they *tell* me?"

"They must have had their reasons."

With a gentle swoop, he carried her to the recliner, settled with her in his lap and tucked her head beneath his chin. He stroked her hair, and his tenderness opened the floodgate of her tears.

In her confused state, she didn't know if she cried

for her sudden loss of identity or her imminent separation from Dylan, whose strength she leaned on now.

"I *hated* it."

She swallowed a sob. "Hated what?"

"Having to tell you." He tucked a strand of hair behind her ear and set off a resonating tingle that vibrated across her shoulders.

"I might *not* be Jasmine's sister."

"There's a good chance you are."

Silently she berated herself for rushing to judgment and assuming the worst. Pushing away from him, she swiped at her eyes with the heel of her hand. "I won't cry."

"Go ahead, if it makes you feel better." He skimmed her cheek with his knuckles. The tender compassion in his eyes threatened to launch her tears again.

"I won't cry." She grappled for control. "It's nonproductive."

His soft chuckle surprised her.

"What's so funny?"

His smile held no derision. "You are."

"Thanks for hitting a girl while she's down."

"I was thinking how unchanging you are, pragmatic, tenacious, resilient. You feel stunned now, but you won't let this defeat you."

She wished she had his confidence. Sliding her arm around his waist, she nestled her face against his throat and experienced a warm, enveloping calm. "This is part of your job, right?"

"Cuddling attractive young females?" Amused surprise colored his voice.

Without looking at him, she shook her head. "Making people feel safe."

His hand cupped her face, bringing her eyes level with his. "You're not safe with me."

Before she could breathe, his mouth covered hers. The pressure of his lips drove hers apart, lengthening and deepening the kiss, igniting a fire within her, a frenzied flame that leaped to match the feverish heat she felt in him.

With a hunger too long unsatisfied, she melted against him and ran her hands over his face, broad shoulders and the hard, sinewy muscles of his arms. Need, wild and wanton, drove out every conscious thought but her yearning to meld her body with his in blood-pounding abandon.

When he slipped his hands beneath her blouse and his fingers skimmed her breasts, a flash of heat, like summer lightning, zigzagged all the way to her belly. The hard, hot evidence of his desire pulsed beneath her thighs.

As abruptly as he'd begun, he dropped his hands and lifted his head. "We'd better stop."

His sudden halt jarred her and restored her reason. He was right. They'd been down this road, and although the journey had been glorious, heartache lay at its end.

She wriggled from his lap and adjusted her clothes.

"Your parents will be here any minute."

Standing beside her, he straightened the sling that supported her bandaged arm. His breathing rattled in her ears, as rapid and ragged as her own.

She stepped away to remove herself from temptation. Not only did she want him in the most primal way, she loved him beyond reason.

God help me, I will never stop loving him.

A sensation of terrible loss choked her with its magnitude. His attitude about marriage and commitment hadn't changed. She'd almost lost her son and her life. And now, in a few minutes, she might discover that the couple she believed had given her birth weren't her real parents after all.

"Everything's going to work out, Heather." His voice, as warm and comforting as his arms, caressed her. "I promise."

He closed the gap between them and lowered his head to claim her lips again. His kiss was longer, deeper and infinitely more tender than the one before. Its potency weakened her knees and bolstered her flagging hope.

With a shuddering breath, he broke away. "I promise."

She wanted to ask how he intended to keep that promise, but the crunch of tires on the driveway announced her parents' arrival. Torn between happiness at seeing them and fear of what they might tell her, she walked outside to greet them.

Her father climbed from the driver's side of his new Saturn and, with the courtesy Heather always associated with him, hustled to open her mother's door. As they approached her, changes, evident in just the few short weeks since Easter vacation, struck her.

Both would soon be seventy, and although they followed a healthy routine vigorously, especially since her father's heart attack, they couldn't fend off forever the effects of aging. Her mother's shoulders were more stooped, and her father's hair had turned noticeably whiter.

"Oh, Heather." Her mother's lips trembled at the sight of her. "We were so worried."

Bending to embrace her mother with her uninjured arm, Heather wondered why she'd never questioned how little she resembled either of her parents. Tall, slender, with light brown hair and green eyes, she looked nothing like Barbara or David Taylor, both short and stocky with dark eyes, and hair that had been coal black before age dulled its color.

"I'm fine, Mother."

"But your arm?" Anxiety glittered in her mother's deep-set eyes.

"Once the stitches are out, it'll be good as new. Hi, Daddy."

Careful of her injured arm, her father squeezed her in a bear hug. "You look great, pumpkin."

Heather hugged him back and smiled. His steady optimism had always provided a welcome buffer to her mother's chronic apprehension.

They climbed the porch steps, and Dylan opened the front door. "Hello, Barbara, David. You must be tired from your trip."

In the living room, her parents sat side by side on Dylan's long sofa. Heather took the recliner, and Dylan straddled a hassock.

Her father cleared his throat. "We appreciated your call, Dylan. Heather was trying to spare us worry by keeping us in the dark about the threats to her and Chip—" he flashed her a smile to show he understood "—but now that we know, we want to help."

Dylan also shot Heather a glance, encouraging her to inquire about her birth parents. She knew she had to ask, but the question lodged in her throat.

Her mother came to her rescue. "Tell her, David."

Her father took her mother's hand, as if for strength. "It's a long drive from Fort Lauderdale, so your mother and I had plenty of time to talk. When Dylan called yesterday and told us about the threats, we knew we couldn't keep our secret any longer."

"We spent the entire trip," her mother added, "trying to decide the best way to say it."

"There's no easy way, pumpkin," said her father, a telltale moisture glistening in his eyes, "except to come right out with it."

Her mother nodded. "Especially when the knowledge might save yours and Chip's lives."

"We're not your natural parents." Her father's expression begged forgiveness.

Disclosing the twenty-five-year-old secret was obvious agony for her parents, and although Heather expected her father's confession, his words struck like a hammer blow.

Thanks to Dylan's preparing her for their news, she received it without falling to pieces. She communicated her gratitude with a bittersweet smile.

He returned her glance with a smoldering look that brought a flush to her cheeks. Since the day after her attack, a subtle but significant change had occurred in their relationship. The invisible wall he had always raised between them, even in the heat of lovemaking, had disappeared by degrees, and a vital intimacy had taken its place.

In spite of the joy this new rapport gave her, she knew better than to hope for permanent commitment. Her emotions were already raw from learning of her adoption. She refused to risk more grief by wanting what, even now, she doubted he was willing to give.

She turned to her parents and prodded gently. "Maybe you should tell me the whole story."

"We wanted you so much," her mother said with a quiver in her voice. "We'd been married fifteen years, and in spite of all our efforts, I couldn't conceive."

"The older we grew," her father added, "the less likely an adoption agency was to assign us a child. The ad in our local paper was a godsend."

"Ad? By an adoption agency?" Dylan asked.

"No," her father said, "from an unnamed attorney with a blind post office box. Applicants who wanted to adopt a child were to send their qualifications."

"The man who called on us was very nice," her mother continued. "He said he was an attorney but refused to give his name. If we wanted the baby, he said, everything was to be transacted in the strictest secrecy."

As she spoke, her mother appeared to relax. Perhaps the fact that Heather had accepted the news without hysterics had made the telling easier.

Dylan raised an eyebrow. "Didn't the secrecy make you suspicious?"

"You bet," her dad answered without hesitation, "but the lawyer assured us everything was in order, that secrecy was only to protect the baby's mother."

Her mother nodded. "He told a very touching story about a wealthy young socialite, pregnant as the result of an indiscriminate affair. She was able to hide her pregnancy from her husband, out of the country on an extended business trip, and wanted her child adopted before his return."

"We could adopt," her father continued, "only if we agreed never to reveal to you that you had been adopted. Your natural mother, the lawyer said, wanted to insure that you wouldn't show up on her doorstep and ruin her marriage."

Her mother shook her head. "And we believed him, because he was so charming and articulate. And because we wanted you so desperately."

Tears blurred Heather's vision. "And that's why you never told me?"

She nodded. "We were afraid you might rush off searching for your real parents, and if you found them, they'd break your heart."

Heather rose and moved to the sofa between them. "*You* are my true parents. Nothing will ever alter that."

Her mom and dad embraced her, then her mother shed a few tears. When her father had yanked his handkerchief from his pocket and blown his nose, Dylan spoke.

"What did this attorney look like?"

"Slender, average height, glasses," her mother said, "and his hair was starting to thin."

"We never learned his name," her father added. "The only other information we had was from his car's license plate. The tag was from this county."

"Surely the attorney isn't the one who's threatening Heather and Chip?'' her mother said. "He seemed like such a nice young man.''

Dylan scowled. "If he's who I think he is, he's serving a life sentence for kidnapping and attempted murder.''

Shock and dismay registered on her parents' faces.

"Tell them,'' Heather said to Dylan, "everything you told me about Jasmine and her family.''

While Dylan repeated the story, Heather absorbed details she had been too stunned to grasp the first time. His account of Lily's imprisonment and stolen baby brought tears to her parents' eyes.

"You believe Heather is Lily's daughter, Jasmine's sister?'' her father asked when Dylan finished.

"The secrecy of Heather's adoption, her age and the matching birthmarks are strong circumstantial proof,'' Dylan said, "but we'll need hard evidence to be certain.''

"How can we help?'' her father asked. "We'll stay as long as you need us.''

Heather blanched at his offer. As living witnesses to her illegal adoption, her parents could be in as much danger as she was.

Judging from the furrows between his eyebrows, she suspected Dylan's thoughts were running in the same direction.

"You could be the most help with Chip,'' he said. "He's with my folks up on the river. I know they'd appreciate a hand, and they'd enjoy seeing you again, too.''

Heather could have hugged him. Chip would make her mother forget her worries, and with her folks at the river under Frank and Jake's watchful eyes, she wouldn't have to worry about their safety.

"How about some lunch first?" Dylan suggested. "Then I'll draw you a map to the river cottage."

HEATHER WAVED GOODBYE from the driveway as her folks pulled away. Dylan hovered close by, apparently alert to the possibility of another attack. When she headed inside, she caught sight of Sid Bullock, parked in an old Plymouth down the street.

"Is he there because of me?"

Dylan hurried her into the house and locked the door. "Sid doesn't take kindly to people trying to kill the citizens he's sworn to protect. He's anxious to get his hands on your attacker."

She lifted her hand to his cheek. "Thanks for keeping my folks safe."

His big hand covered hers, and he touched her palm to his lips. "I've always liked your folks, but I doubt, under the circumstances, the feeling's mutual."

She frowned. "What circumstances?"

"Chip. They know I'm his father. Don't they wonder why I didn't marry you?"

Remembering the quarrel the night she'd told them she was expecting, she shuddered. Her father had threatened to go after Dylan with a shotgun, until she'd explained that he didn't know about her pregnancy and had convinced them why she didn't want to tell him. "They understand."

Pain flashed in the mahogany depths of his eyes, and he dropped her hand.

To break the tension, she changed the subject.

"Shouldn't we tell Rand and Jasmine what we suspect?"

"Later. First, you're going to rest."

She couldn't argue. Even if she'd been in top physical condition, learning of her adoption would have drained her emotionally. She wanted to sleep for a week. But when she lay down in Dylan's darkened bedroom, her mind churned with questions.

Was she really Talbot and Lily Moore's missing child? If so, she had a sister, Jasmine, and three half brothers, T.J., Art and Blain Moore. If she was their kin, why was she such a threat that one of them wanted her and her son dead? Was the motive money, as Dylan believed? Or did the person who'd knifed her have nothing to do with the Moores?

Unable to find answers, she fell asleep.

Shadows were lengthening when she awakened, and the aroma of tomatoes, garlic and basil drifted down the hall. Dylan was cooking his special *pomodoro* sauce that she hadn't tasted in more than two years.

Her rest restored her energy, and after a spaghetti supper and a call to Chip at the river, she sipped a cup of cappuccino while Dylan loaded the dishwasher.

"Feel up to visiting Rand and Jasmine now?" He placed the last dish in the rack and closed the door.

"I think so. I can't get used to the idea that I might have brothers and a sister." Butterflies dive-bombed in her stomach at the thought.

"And Chip has uncles, another aunt, and another set of grandparents." He dried his hands on a kitchen towel.

"Don't say any more, please. The possibilities are overwhelming."

He placed his palms flat on the table and leaned toward her, his eyes hot, his voice gritty. "Don't worry. They won't be able to help loving you."

She lowered her gaze so he couldn't see hope flaring in her eyes as she waited for his answer. "Speaking from personal experience?"

When he took too long to reply, she raised her head and caught the gleam of mischief in his crooked grin.

"Yeah," he said, "they couldn't help loving me, either."

She stifled a laugh. "You're impossible."

"That's what my mama always told me."

"Your mama was right."

"I'm discovering my mama was right about a lot of things, including you."

If he looked at her like that another minute, they would never leave the house tonight. "Aren't Rand and Jasmine expecting us?"

"You're right." He shook his head as if coming out of a trance.

She followed him into the living room. He removed his keys from a shelf by the door, slipped one off the ring and handed it to her.

"I'll turn on the outside lights and check the car. When I give you the all clear, come out and lock the front door behind you."

His precautions brought back vivid memories of the attack in his driveway. She watched from the window until he'd inspected the bushes near the drive, circled the car and motioned for her to join him. As she locked the door and scampered to the car, she spotted the dark shadow of Sid Bullock's Plymouth across the street.

She waved to the detective as Dylan drove away. "Doesn't he ever sleep?"

"Sid? Not if he's on a case."

"When does he eat?"

"One of the guys on patrol drops off coffee and sandwiches when he's on surveillance."

"How—" Her question died in her throat as Dylan slammed on his brakes to avoid a car that darted in front of them at the intersection. The other vehicle's engine gunned, and it speeded off in the direction they were headed. The Jeep's headlights briefly illuminated the driver.

"It's him!" she cried. "The man who kidnapped Chip."

Dylan stomped the accelerator and took off after the black Chevy Blazer. He passed her his phone and shouted a number. "Call Bullock. Tell him we're in hot pursuit, headed for the interstate."

She punched in the number with shaking fingers. Dylan tailed the rocketing vehicle along several blocks and followed it up the interstate entrance ramp.

"We caught the bastard by surprise," Dylan said.

"I can't get through to Bullock. Some kind of interference."

"High tension lines. We're almost clear of them. Keep trying."

The Jeep flew onto the deserted interstate, close behind the Blazer.

She lifted the phone to try her call again, and the

Jeep lurched downward, tossing her toward the windshield until her seat belt yanked her back. Metal screamed, showers of fiery sparks spewed from beneath the front of the vehicle, and a tire bounced past her window.

Dylan wrestled with the wheel, and the Jeep bucked and pitched for endless seconds before screeching to a halt on the shoulder of the highway.

"Are you okay?" he asked. "You didn't hurt your arm?"

"I'm okay. What happened?" Her voice shook with the rest of her.

"We lost the right front tire."

"How can you lose a tire?"

"Someone must have loosened the lug nuts."

"Why?"

"To stop us and create an easy target. Running into our kidnapper wasn't coincidence after all."

He stared through the windshield at the highway ahead, and she followed his gaze. Several hundred yards in front of them, the Blazer crossed the median, made a U-turn and speeded toward them.

Dylan unfastened his seat belt and pulled his gun. "Get on the floor in back and stay down."

Chapter Thirteen

From the opposite lane of the highway, the Blazer swerved onto the wide grassy median directly across from them. With the Jeep immobilized without its right front tire, Dylan had no means for their escape.

He groped along the floorboards for the phone, thrown from Heather's hand when the axle hit the pavement. His fingers closed over its outer case, and he tossed it to her in the back seat. "Call 911."

A quick scan of the four-lane highway showed several cars traveling in the opposite direction, unaware or uncaring of his plight. No headlights glimmered on the dark road behind the Jeep. In the back seat Heather talked to the emergency operator, but help could be a long time coming.

Lunging across the front seats, he reached to open the passenger door, but the wail of an approaching siren stopped him. Raising his head warily, he peered through the rear window and grinned.

Flashing blue lights were bearing down on them. Fast.

The Blazer's driver had apparently seen the lights, too. The black vehicle bounced off the median onto the pavement near the Jeep and accelerated away from the approaching police car. Seconds later, Sid Bullock's Plymouth barreled past, leaving the Jeep quaking in its vortex.

Dylan climbed from the Jeep and helped Heather out of the back seat. "You okay?"

Her face was drawn and pale in the moonlight, but she nodded and handed him the phone.

"We'll need a tow truck," he told the operator. "And alert police south of us to be on the lookout for a late-model black Chevy Blazer exiting the interstate."

AN HOUR LATER, Dylan and Heather sat in the back seat of Sid's Plymouth and watched the tow truck, orange lights blinking, haul away the Jeep.

"Too bad you lost him," he said to Sid.

"He disappeared into a stream of traffic at the mall. Even with my siren blaring, I couldn't get through fast enough to catch up."

"He was waiting for us." Heather shivered. "He pulled in front of us on purpose, knowing we'd follow."

Sid nodded. "With me watching the house, he had to lure you into the open for another shot at you. He must have loosened the lug nuts on Dylan's tire while the Jeep was parked at the hospital night before last."

"I owe you," Dylan said. "Things could have turned nasty if you hadn't shown up when you did."

"We're still no closer to catching this creep." Sid struck the steering wheel with his fist in frustration, then started the engine and drove onto the highway.

"He smeared mud on his tag, so I can't trace him through the Department of Motor Vehicles."

"After I've talked with Rand Sinclair," Dylan said, "maybe we'll have a better idea who we're dealing with."

He pulled Heather closer. Someone was determined to kill her. He was just as determined to catch the assailant and throw his sorry butt in jail.

"THAT'S EVERYTHING that's happened until now." Dylan finished his account of Chip's kidnapping and the attacks on Heather, including the one less than two hours ago on the interstate.

Rand reclined against the back of the leather sofa with his arm around his wife. Even in the final stages of pregnancy, Jasmine managed to look gorgeous and at ease.

While telling his story, Dylan had shifted his gaze between Heather and Jasmine. He couldn't understand why he hadn't noted the resemblance before. Jasmine's long hair was straight and blond, and Heather's honey-hued curls were short. Jasmine's eyes were emerald, while the green in Heather's was the earthy color of moss, flecked with gold and brown. But both women were tall and slender, their hands graceful and elegant, and their profiles identical.

Before, Dylan had attributed his aching discontent whenever he was around Jasmine to the contrast of his solitary state with Rand's married happiness. Now he realized that Jasmine's subtle resemblance to Heather had activated his longing for the woman he loved.

"We can't be certain we're sisters until DNA tests are completed," Heather was saying.

Jasmine cradled her belly and the child she carried and smiled. "Anybody not blind in both eyes can tell we're related. When there was just Aunt Daisy and me, I yearned for family. Last year, I found my mother and father, as well as my brothers, and now I have a sister."

Rand cleared his throat, and when she looked at him, he raised an eyebrow. "What about me?"

Her face crinkled into a teasing smile. "*You* are responsible for my months of nausea and waddling like a duck. Don't push your luck."

Rand kissed the tip of her nose.

Dylan, remembering how Heather had carried Chip all those months and delivered him alone, experienced a spasm of regret.

"Shouldn't we tell Mom and Dad about this?" Jasmine asked Rand.

"I'm happy to have a sister-in-law," he said with a nod to Heather, "but it might be best to wait until blood tests confirm your kinship before telling Lily and Talbot."

"I agree," Heather said. "Let's find who's trying to kill me first."

Dylan leaned forward. "I figure someone who knows that Heather is Talbot's daughter is behind Chip's kidnapping and the attacks on her."

"Charles Wilcox is the prime suspect," Rand said. "He unquestionably is the one who kidnapped Heather when she was a baby and gave her to the Taylors."

"Charles is in prison for life," Dylan said.

"Then it has to be someone else." Rand flung his hands wide in a gesture of frustration. "But who? And for what reason?"

Jasmine narrowed her green eyes. "Money."

"Your father is a very wealthy man," Dylan said. "His estate, split between four children, would make each a multimillionaire."

"And Heather makes five," Rand said. "Her existence, and Chip's, would mean a smaller piece of Talbot's estate for everyone."

"It's ridiculous," Jasmine said, "to be talking about Daddy's estate. He's only in his fifties and in excellent health. Besides, I don't want his money, I want my father around to enjoy his grandchildren."

"What about your—our brothers?" Heather asked.

"T.J. and Art love Talbot as much as the rest of us," Rand said. "They'd never do anything to hurt him."

"Not even for a bigger inheritance?" Dylan asked.

Rand shook his head. "They enjoy their work in the company and are well paid. Neither has money problems or has ever shown greed. Besides, T.J.'s been in Detroit the past week for a builder's convention, and Art spends all his free time with his fiancée."

"Blain blamed Talbot for divorcing his mother," Dylan reminded him.

"Blain is in France with Irene," Jasmine said. "When Daddy divorced her, he gave her the vineyard he'd recently bought, and she and Blain are running it. Their wine produces a good income. Between the winery's profits and Daddy's settlement, Irene is a rich woman."

"Some people never have enough money." Dylan frowned. "And if Talbot's money isn't the motive behind these attacks, what is?"

"Revenge?" Heather suggested.

Rand looked thoughtful. "Maybe Irene didn't take the divorce and settlement as amicably as we thought."

Jasmine shook her head. "From everything we've heard, she's perfectly happy in France."

Dylan stood, shoved his hands in his pockets and paced the Oriental carpet of Rand and Jasmine's spacious living room. "Detective Cramer in St. Pete has already eliminated every possible suspect who might have a grudge against Heather. Her parents could think of no one with ill will toward them. Unless some psychotic wacko has chosen Heather for some unknown reason, that leaves only her connection to Talbot as motive."

"You think an insane person could be behind all this?" Jasmine asked with a shudder.

"It's possible," Dylan said, "but unlikely. If Heather was chosen at random, as closely as she's been guarded, her assailant would have selected a more accessible target by now. Her relationship to Talbot has to be the key."

"Charles Wilcox," Jasmine said, "is the only one who *knows* she's Daddy's daughter."

Rand nodded. "Killing Talbot's daughter and grandson would mean more money for Charles's nephews when Talbot dies. Charles also blames his imprisonment on Talbot and Lily, so he might consider killing the daughter they're searching for fitting revenge. As twisted as Charles's mind is, he could be planning to tell the Moores that Heather's their daughter—after she's murdered.''

Heather's eyes clouded with confusion. "But Charles is in prison. How can he harm us from there?"

Dylan stopped pacing. "He's allowed mail, phone calls and visitors. With his access to other criminals, finding and hiring a hit man wouldn't be a problem.''

"Charles won't help us," Rand said. "He refused to tell Talbot what he'd done with Lily's baby. He'll be less likely to rat on a professional murderer who might have friends in the same prison.''

"He doesn't have to *tell* us anything." Dylan grinned with satisfaction. "Everything Charles does—visitors, calls and letters, friendships within the prison—is monitored. If he made the contact, information from the prison records should lead us to Heather's attacker.''

"You'll check with the prison?" Rand asked.

"Right." Dylan glanced at Heather and noted the violet shadows beneath her eyes. "But first, I'm taking Heather home. She needs her rest.''

Rand and Jasmine walked them to the front door.

Jasmine hugged Heather, not an easy task when she was eight months pregnant and Heather had a bandaged arm, and kissed her cheek. "Welcome to the family, sis. After Dylan catches his bad guy, we'll have a reunion celebration that'll knock your socks off.''

Heather returned Jasmine's hug, then walked with Dylan to Sid's Plymouth in the front drive. Dylan settled her in the back seat and climbed in front with Sid.

"Well," Sid said, "did you get that lead you were hoping for?"

"Uh-huh. If you don't mind a late night, I'll explain after I place a call to the warden at Starke."

"About what?"

"Charles Wilcox."

"The guy who tried to kill Jasmine and Talbot Moore last year?"

Dylan nodded.

Sid flicked his gaze from the street to Dylan. "I got a feeling there's a lot you haven't told me."

Dylan glanced at Heather, already asleep on the back seat. "It's a long story. Come in for coffee at my house, and I'll fill you in."

DYLAN SHIFTED ON THE SOFA, opened his eyes and squinted in the blinding sunlight spilling through his living room window. Sitting up, he stretched and rubbed his aching shoulder where he'd slept on it wrong.

Voices drifted from the kitchen, and he pushed to his feet. Sid's car was out front, where he'd left it last night, and the fragrant aroma of coffee drifted through the house.

Dylan padded past his open bedroom door and noted the neatly made bed. In the kitchen, he found Heather sitting at the table and Sid serving breakfast.

Her eyes met Dylan's, and a cramp of longing closed around his heart. He wanted to see Heather every morning when he awoke, to share breakfast with her, to hear the sweet music of her laughter and bask in the radiance of her smile.

"Feeling better?" he asked.

"A hundred percent." She lifted her bandaged arm and beamed a smile that would thaw an iceberg. "I don't need the sling anymore."

Love, powerful as a tsunami, washed over him. Threatened as she'd been, other women might cower and snivel, but Heather had never allowed adversity to squelch her invincible spirit. To keep from touching her, he settled in a chair at the opposite end of the table.

"How about you?" Sid poured Dylan's coffee. "Get any sleep?"

"Yeah, thanks."

Dylan sipped the strong, hot brew, remembering his long talk with Sid after Heather had fallen asleep last night. Sid had listened to his summary of Heather's connection with Talbot Moore and agreed with the theory that Charles Wilcox was somehow involved.

While Sid grabbed a few hours' sleep on the living room sofa, Dylan had called Starke and talked to a prison official who promised to collect the data Dylan requested. Later, when Sid awakened to stand watch, Dylan caught some sleep. They both needed to stay alert. The would-be killer was getting desperate.

Sid, his coffee mug almost hidden in his beefy hand, leaned his bulky frame against the counter. "I called the station. One of the guys is bringing you an unmarked car from the motor pool until your Jeep's repaired."

The buzz of the telephone interrupted Dylan's thanks. He jumped up and snatched the receiver off the wall phone. "Wade, here."

Warden O'Brien's hearty voice reverberated in his ear. Dylan listened carefully to the man's report, thanked him and hung up.

"Well?" Heather asked. "What did he say?"

Attempting to assimilate the significance of O'Brien's findings, Dylan sank back into his chair. "In the short time Charles Wilcox has been at Starke, he's corresponded with only two people, his sister Irene and her son Blain."

"Phone calls?" Sid asked.

"None."

"Visitors?"

"Only one, a few days ago. Irene Moore."

Heather winced in surprise. "But Irene is in France."

"Maybe." Dylan fixed her with a steady look as pieces of the puzzle tumbled into place. "She visited Charles the day before Chip was kidnapped."

"Looks like," Sid suggested, "this Irene isn't as content with her divorce as the Sinclairs seem to think. Hell hath no fury like a woman scorned, remember?"

Dylan nodded grimly. "Check to see if Irene returned to France. If she didn't, we'd better find her and bring her in for questioning."

HEATHER ADJUSTED her sunglasses, a part of her disguise, against the glare of the afternoon sun, and peered through the car window. In exasperation, she jerked the straw hat from her head and ran her fingers through her hair.

"How much longer?"

Dylan, wearing a Blue Jays cap and aviator lenses, eased the Ford LTD around a corner. "Are you tired?"

"After eight solid hours of driving up and down every street in Dolphin Bay?" She couldn't keep the edge from her voice. Her wounded arm ached and her nerves unraveled further by the minute. "Why should I be tired?"

"Because you've been through hell the past few days." His comforting tone soothed her as much as his strong fingers, massaging the back of her neck.

She regretted her petulance. "Do you think we'll find Irene?"

"Every department in the county is searching for her and the two vehicles she's been seen in. Sid and his detectives are calling hotels and motels in case she's registered under her real name."

"In a resort area like this, she could be at any one of thousands of places. Finding her could take days."

"Patience. That's what police work is all about."

She shifted her scrutiny from the passing landscape to Dylan. He exuded calm, from the shadowed planes of his face and his relaxed posture to the tranquil brown of his eyes. Easygoing, Dylan had patience in spades and was slow to anger, even when provoked. A wonderful quality in a husband.

She quashed her longing for the unattainable and reminded herself that Dylan's involvement in her case was based on two things: his desire to protect his son and his dedication to his job. Once he caught Irene, Heather wouldn't see him again.

"I doubt Irene is staying at a motel or hotel," he said.

"You mean we've been wasting our time?"

"We've checked every hotel with a parking garage with no luck. If she's smart, she rented some place with a two-car garage where she hides her vehicles."

"Then how will we find her?"

"She has to come out sometime. Every officer in the county is on the alert for her and those vehicles. It may take time, but we'll get her."

Time?

Heather couldn't spend much more time with Dylan without losing her mind. Being near him was an exquisite torture. She sighed, pressed her forehead against the cool glass of the window and yearned for Chip. His sunny disposition had helped her through many a bad time in the past. When this nightmare was over, she'd no longer have Dylan, but at least she'd have her son. *His* son.

"That was a heavy sigh," Dylan said.

"I was thinking about Chip. I hope he's not missing me too much."

"We've done enough today. I'll head back to the house, and you can give him a call. Maybe hearing his voice will make you feel better."

But it didn't.

Back in Dylan's kitchen, she hung up the phone after her conversation with Chip. He hadn't cried, but she'd heard the plaintive tone in his precious voice.

She craved to hold him. He was so small, and he didn't understand why his mommy wasn't with him.

Her stomach knotted, her throat ached and her eyes filled with tears. She wanted to snuggle with him before bedtime as she'd done every night since his birth—until a few days ago.

"You miss him, don't you." Dylan moved toward her, draped his arms over her shoulders and pulled her close.

"It's like losing a part of myself." Surrendering to his solace, she buried her face in his shirt and inhaled the earthy, male scent of him.

He closed his arms around her and breathed against her temple. "I'm sorry."

"For what?"

"For the things that have happened."

"The attacks?"

"Those, too, but mainly for how things turned out between us."

"There is no *us*." Her old anger flared like a Roman candle.

He held her tight. "For that, I'm sorriest of all."

At his words, her heart skipped, her pulse revved, and she fought back fresh tears.

"Me, too," she whispered against his chest.

He lifted her face, and she glimpsed the passion glowing in his eyes before he covered her mouth with his. At the contact, an explosiveness erupted between them, as if the air had ignited. Helpless against her need, she abandoned herself to his kisses, to the ravenous exploration of his lips and tongue, the nip of his teeth at her neck.

Winding her fingers through his hair, she nestled

closer and molded her body to his, while his large, strong hands caressed her, electrifying every nerve ending they touched. Like dry ground to a soaking rain, she opened herself to his raw and sensuous power, drinking in the sweet, remembered taste of his kisses, absorbing the river of heat flowing from his fingers.

A warning sounded in the back of her mind, a reminder that commitment, not transitory pleasure, was what she needed. She pulled back, but when Dylan swept her into his arms and carried her into the bedroom, passion numbed her consciousness, curbing all awareness except how much she wanted him.

He toppled her onto the bed, covered her with his body and pushed aside her clothes in his haste. With shaking fingers, she helped peel away the layers of fabric between them. At the contact of his naked flesh with hers, two years of repressed desire burst free, magnifying her need.

"Now," she begged. "Please."

He drove into her with a force that took her breath away. The fury of his pent-up longing kindled her response, stoked her passion and consumed her in a conflagration of sensations that drove out all consciousness except the two of them, wrapped in each other's arms.

A while later, he shifted off her but kept his arm around her, drawing her close to his side. His lips moved against her forehead. "I love you, Heather. I will always love you."

Floating in blissful tranquillity, she realized, for

now, love was enough. If commitment never came, at least she'd had tonight.

With that consoling thought, when he drew her atop him, she went gladly into his arms.

THE SQUAWK AND STATIC of the two-way radio on the bedside table roused Dylan from a deep slumber. His watch read two in the morning.

He snatched up the radio and stepped into the hall to avoid waking Heather. "Wade here."

"We're out front." Sam's voice crackled loudly. "And we've got her."

"Irene?"

"Ten-four."

"I'll be right there."

Dylan dragged on jeans, jammed his feet into a pair of deck shoes and tugged a shirt over his head. With a final glance at Heather, her unforgettable face peaceful in sleep, her naked curves tempting beneath the thin cover of the sheet, he slipped from the room and made his way to the front lawn.

He spotted Sid Bullock's massive silhouette at the edge of his drive. "Where is she?"

Sid jerked a thumb over his shoulder. "Jeb's got her in the back seat of my car."

Surveying the street, Dylan caught sight of a white Mercedes two houses away. "What happened?"

"Jeb and I were watching your house when the Mercedes pulled up and the driver turned off its lights. When she stepped out of the car, we jumped out and nabbed her."

"I want to talk to her."

Sid grimaced in the moonlight. "Lotsa luck."

Dylan's jaw ached from clenching his teeth against the fury raging inside him. He strode to Sid's car and yanked open the back door.

Jeb Greenlea climbed out. "She won't say anything. Says she wants a lawyer."

Dylan acknowledged his statement with a curt nod and slid onto the back seat. The dim interior light illuminated a tall, slender woman with disarrayed blond hair and a wild look in her eyes. Her hands fluttered around her as if they had a mind of their own.

"Dylan," she exclaimed in a breathless voice, "thank God."

"I'm the last person you should want to see." His voice rasped like a file against metal.

Her hands grew suddenly still. "Why?"

"Because it's *my* son you kidnapped, and the woman *I* love that you almost killed."

"But I didn't!" Her hysterical cry vibrated in the humid night air.

Craving to shake the truth out of her, he leaned toward her. Only the rigid discipline of his training restrained him. "Then why was *your* car used to kidnap Chip? Why was *your* car in the alley behind Heather's house? Why did *you* go to her school looking for her?"

She launched her trembling fingers into motion again, tugging her hair, smoothing her skirt, twisting her diamond-heavy rings. Her gaze bounced wildly, landing everywhere except on him.

He thrust his face inches from hers and demanded with a growl, "Why, Irene? Was it revenge? Or money? So your sons will get more of Talbot's inheritance?''

Stillness settled over her again and, when she spoke, her voice was a hesitant whisper. "I wanted to warn her.''

"What?'' Her answer wasn't the response he expected.

"I went to Heather's school to warn her.'' Her words spilled out in a tumble. "Before—''

She clamped her lips together and looked away.

Tears slipped from her eyes and caught in the fine lines of her face, but Dylan felt no sympathy. As long as he'd known Irene, beginning in the days he and Rand had played together as young boys, this helpless, insecure female had depended on others, clinging to the people around her like a parasitic plant.

Her brother Charles had imprisoned Lily, the woman Talbot loved, so Talbot would marry his sister. Irene had allowed Charles and her sons to fight her battles for her, had made Talbot's life a living hell, and now she had tried to kill Heather and Chip.

She would need more than tears to gain Dylan's sympathy. He forced a gentleness he didn't feel into his voice. "Why are you here tonight?''

She turned her head and met his eyes. The movement dislodged her tears, and they tracked down her bare cheeks. "I was following Blain.''

Dylan blinked in surprise. "I thought Blain was still in France. What's he doing here?''

As soon as the words left his mouth, the final piece of the puzzle dropped into place, and the horror of the answer spurred him into action. He dived out the open door and hit the ground running.

The explosion ripped the night and knocked him backward. As he fell, flames erupted, shattering the windows of his house.

He was too late.

"Heather!"

Echoes from the blast drowned his cry.

Chapter Fourteen

Flames licked the night and thick plumes of foul smoke surged skyward, smothering the stars. Dylan scrambled frantically to his feet and raced toward his house.

He hurdled the porch steps and flung open the front door, but a backdraft of searing flames drove him away. Choking in the acrid, superheated air, he careered around the corner to his bedroom window.

Refusing to believe Heather was dead, he smashed the windowpane with his elbow and wrenched the lock open. He raised the sash, hoisted himself over the sill and plunged into the pitch-black, smoke-filled room.

"Heather!"

He could see nothing but flames outlining the closed door to the hall. Around him, the house crackled and popped as the fire devoured it. In the darkness, he fumbled for his bearings.

"I'm here. I can't see which way to go."

Her voice and sharp, hacking cough led him in the right direction. He stumbled against the edge of the bed and gathered her in his arms.

"I've got you," he said. "Hold on."

Another spasm of coughing was her only reply.

Crouching to catch breathable air, he turned and headed for what he hoped was the window, but in the inky darkness of black smoke and blinding fumes, he lost his sense of direction.

Erupting with a whoosh, the interior wall of the bedroom burst into flames. Heather tightened her arms around his neck.

"Dylan!" Jeb Greenlea's voice penetrated the holocaust. "Are you in there?"

Following Jeb's shouts, Dylan located the open window and lowered Heather, a sheet wrapped around her, into Jeb's arms. As Dylan vaulted over the sill, the ceiling crashed to the floor in the room behind him.

On the ground a safe distance from the flames, Dylan took Heather from Jeb. "Thanks."

Jeb smiled and socked Dylan's shoulder. "You would have done the same for me."

Dylan glanced at Heather, her face streaked with soot. "You okay?"

"As soon as I clear the smoke from my lungs." She gasped a constricted breath, and a fit of coughing racked her again.

Dylan pulled her close and suppressed the sob rising in his throat. He'd almost lost her. Another minute longer before he had reached her, and she would have perished when the ceiling caved in.

The scream of approaching sirens drowned the hiss and rumble of the burning house, and three neon yellow Dolphin Bay fire trucks rolled to a stop behind him.

"Where's Sid?" Jeb asked suddenly.

Dylan swung his gaze to Sid's empty car, then across the crowd of neighbors who had gathered along the street. "And Irene?"

A paramedic approached. Dylan left Heather in the paramedic's care, then broke into a run, with Jeb alongside, around the blazing house to the backyard.

He skidded to a stop as a bulky figure emerged from the smoke with a bundle in his arms.

"Irene tried to force her way in the back door," Sid said. "I had to knock her out with a punch to the jaw to keep her from throwing herself in the flames."

"She attempted suicide?" Jeb asked.

Sid shook his head. "She kept screaming for Blain. I think her son's inside."

Dylan peered through the smoke at what had once been his home. The roof had collapsed, and only a few blackened timbers still stood beneath the stream of water firemen poured on the ruins.

If Blain had been inside, he was dead now.

For the first time, Dylan felt sympathy for Irene. No one should have to lose a son in an inferno like that. Overwhelmed by his sudden need for Heather, he wheeled and sprinted toward the street.

He found her, the sheet draped around her like a Roman toga, sitting in the back of the paramedic's vehicle, inhaling oxygen through a mask. She had never looked more beautiful, even with her face smeared with ashes and her eyes red-rimmed from smoke.

When she saw him, she smiled with a brightness that drove the breath from his fume-seared lungs.

"You saved my life."

"No." He wrapped his arms around her. "I saved *my* life."

She lifted her head and appraised him with a puzzled look. "But you were outside when the fire started."

"*You*—" he brushed his lips across hers "—are my life."

She clasped her arms around his waist. "I don't know how to thank you for risking your life for me."

If she kept smiling at him like that, he wouldn't be responsible for his actions. "If you insist on showing gratitude, I have something in mind."

"What?"

He bobbed his head toward the watching crowd. "Later."

SCRUBBED CLEAN OF SOOT and the acrid odor of smoke, and dressed in clothes borrowed from Jasmine, Heather sat in Rand and Jasmine's living room. Beyond the expanse of French doors, the sun plunged toward the shimmering waters of the Gulf of Mexico.

Although she had napped earlier in the afternoon, exhaustion sapped her strength. In the past forty-eight hours, she had not only learned she was adopted, but a half brother she had never met had almost succeeded in killing her. Now her birth parents, two brothers whom she also had yet to meet, and Rand and Jasmine mourned the loss of Blain Moore and the senseless manner in which he'd died.

Blain was dead, and with him, the danger to her and Chip. Aside from a raspiness in her throat, she had suffered no ill effects from the fire. The only casualty besides Blain was Dylan's house, reduced to ashes.

She glanced at the ormolu clock on the mantel. With Rand and Jasmine, she had been waiting for almost an hour for Dylan's return from the police station, where he had gone to question Irene. Sipping the white wine Rand had served her, Heather tried to ignore the nervous anticipation of his return, which had her entire body tingling.

She'd had all day to replay memories of the previous twenty-four hours, from Dylan's fierce and tender lovemaking to his daring rescue. When he'd agreed to explain later how she could show her thanks for his heroism, she had heard the promise in his voice, seen it shining in his eyes.

Since then, however, he had been tying up the loose ends of his investigation of the crimes against her, and they had shared only a few words in passing.

The solid *thunk* of a car door in the front drive announced his return and sent her already stimulated nerves into a flutter. From across the room, Jasmine shot her an understanding smile and Rand rose to pour Dylan a drink.

When he entered the living room, her breath lodged in her throat. Because the fire had destroyed his other clothes, he had changed into a uniform from his locker at the station. The dark fitted shirt with its gleaming brass insignia and his sharply creased slacks emphasized his lean handsomeness. Her heart swelled with pride, and she had to restrain herself from rushing across the room and flinging herself into his arms.

Time enough for that later, his eyes promised. For

now, she and Rand and Jasmine wanted to hear the details he had learned.

He sank wearily into an armchair and accepted the filled glass from Rand with a nod of thanks.

"How's Irene?" Jasmine asked.

"Sedated," Dylan answered. "Talbot and Lily have taken her to Moore House to look after her."

Jasmine nodded. "Blain was the youngest of the family. Dad's taking his death hard."

Rand's face settled into grim lines. "I blame Charles Wilcox. Blain was his favorite nephew. Charles spoiled him and eventually drove a wedge between him and his father after Talbot and Irene divorced."

Dylan drank a long swallow and set his glass aside. "According to Irene, Charles was behind this entire scheme. When Blain left France without explanation a couple of weeks ago, Irene found a letter from Charles in his room. The letter said Talbot was looking for his missing child and Charles needed Blain's help to keep Talbot from finding her. He warned Blain that if Heather wasn't killed and Talbot discovered that she was his daughter, she'd eventually have claim to a substantial chunk of Blain's inheritance."

"Last night's fire," Jasmine said, "was exactly like the one Charles set last year that destroyed my house and almost killed me."

"Charles taught Blain well," Dylan said. "The arson investigators found the propane tank that caused the explosion, and the gas can Blain used to soak the kitchen and hall. The quick spread of the blaze evidently took him by surprise. They found his body near the back door.''

Heather shuddered. ''Why did Blain kidnap Chip? If he wanted to kill us both, why didn't he just torch my house in the first place?''

''Irene explained,'' Dylan said, ''that, according to Charles's letter, Blain planned to draw you and Chip into the grove and shoot you both, make it look like a random crime. The small ransom would have been an added bonus.''

''And the later shooting and the knife attack?''

''Backup plans that failed.''

Dylan's voice was calm, but Heather noted the muscle ticking in his jaw, a sign of his repressed fury at the attempts on her life.

''The fire was to be a last resort,'' he continued, ''since that modus operandi would point straight to Charles and lead investigators back to Blain.''

Rand shook his head. ''Knowing Charles, he'd planned to convince Blain to do the dirty work. Charles didn't care about the consequences to Blain. His hatred of Talbot was so strong, he probably intended to implicate Blain all along. After all, what could be more painful for a man than his son's murdering his daughter?''

''Poor Daddy,'' Jasmine murmured. ''But at least this cloud has a silver lining.'' She raised her glass to Heather. ''Dad and Mother have found their missing daughter and have a grandson, too. When will I meet my nephew?''

Heather's upcoming reunion with Chip brought a smile to her face. ''Dylan's folks are bringing him back from the river tonight.''

Rand, his expression thoughtful, stood and propped an elbow on the mantel. "What part did Irene play?"

"Besides confusing us?" Dylan said. "When she kept popping up, we didn't know whether we were searching for a man or a woman. After she found the letter and instructions from Charles, she followed Blain to persuade him to give up his vendetta against his father and return to France. She had the address of the house near here where Blain was staying and found him there."

"That explains the switch in cars," Heather said.

"Right," Dylan said. "When Irene took the Mercedes, Blain rented a Blazer. But she couldn't change his mind. In desperation, she visited Charles in prison to beg him to have Blain abandon his plans."

"Charles refused, of course," Rand said.

Dylan nodded. "Irene called Heather's house to warn her, but couldn't reach her. She went to Heather's school and called her parents, trying to locate her. When Irene couldn't find Heather, she turned her attention to Blain, still hoping to convince him to leave Heather alone and return to France."

"Poor Blain." Jasmine shook her head sadly. "He hated Daddy for divorcing Irene. Charles always spoiled Blain, loaning him money, undermining Dad's attempts to make Blain give up his irresponsible life-style and find a steady job."

"According to Irene," Dylan said, "Blain resented having to work so hard at the winery. He hoped, by eliminating Heather, to insure a greater share of Talbot's estate for himself."

"But Talbot's in good health," Rand said. "Blain

couldn't expect to cash in on his inheritance for decades.''

Dylan's expression turned somber. ''That's the part of Charles's plan for Blain we won't tell Talbot. The man's had enough grief already.''

Jasmine glanced from Dylan to Rand with a puzzled look. ''I don't understand.''

Dylan pushed to his feet. ''After Blain had disposed of Heather and Chip, he intended to murder Talbot, too.''

''My God, I can't believe it.'' Jasmine slumped in her chair. Her stunned gaze swept from face to face. ''Daddy must never know. It would kill him.''

''I agree,'' Dylan said. ''Irene has sworn never to divulge Blain's intentions. And I'm sure no one in this room will, either.''

The emotions and revelations in the room battered Heather. She hadn't yet assimilated the drastic changes the past week had brought to her life. Before the kidnapping, she had been lonely but secure. Then she had endured days of terror, only to find them suddenly and violently ended, with herself in the midst of an extended family she hadn't known existed.

As if Jasmine had read her thoughts, she asked, ''When will you meet Mom and Dad?''

Heather set her wineglass aside and stood by Dylan. ''They need time to grieve for Blain. After the funeral, I'll contact them. Right now, I want to see my son.''

Dylan draped his arm across her shoulders. ''Sid's waiting out front. He'll drive us to my parents' house.''

Rand and Jasmine's goodbyes were subdued. They would leave for Moore House to console Talbot and Lily as soon as Heather and Dylan departed.

On the short drive across town, Sid and Dylan discussed the case against Charles Wilcox.

"I spoke with the district attorney," Sid said. "She has high hopes of a guilty verdict under a conspiracy charge."

"What more can they do to him?" Heather asked. "He's already in prison for life."

"I doubt he'll get a death sentence for conspiracy," Dylan explained, "but the judge can arrange that he never gets paroled, even if he lives to be a hundred."

Sid pulled up in front of the Wades' house. The driveway was empty and no light shone from the windows.

"Looks like you beat Frank and Margaret home," Sid said.

"They'll be here soon." Dylan climbed from the front seat and opened the back door for Heather. "Thanks for the ride."

"Give my regards to your father," Sid called before driving away.

As his taillights disappeared down the street, Heather realized she was alone with Dylan for the first time since before the fire. The beauty of the night pierced her with its sweetness. Crickets chirped in the velvet darkness, and jasmine and frangipani from Margaret's garden scented the air. Overhead, palm fronds rustled like stiff paper in the cool gulf breeze.

The perfection of the evening amplified the sadness in her heart. Soon Chip would return, and when he did, the two of them would go home to St. Petersburg. They were safe once more, but with that safety came separation from Dylan. He had said he loved her, and she'd always known he did. What hadn't changed was his aversion to marriage and commitment.

He took her hand, tugged her up the front walk and onto the front porch. Like a sleepwalker, immersed in the sorrow of their approaching farewell, she sank onto the porch swing beside him.

He encircled her shoulders with his arm and set the swing in motion with his foot. ''There's still one mystery I don't have an answer for.''

The beloved heat of him warmed her for the last time. ''I thought Irene answered all your questions.''

''She couldn't help me with this puzzle.''

At the gravity in his voice, she turned to him. His brown eyes gleamed in the darkness, and the set of his jaw signaled the importance of his statement.

''What puzzle?'' she asked breathlessly.

He stopped the swing. ''Why you stopped loving me two years ago.''

''But I didn't!'' The denial escaped before she could stop it.

He grasped her shoulders gently, forcing her to meet his gaze. ''If you loved me, then why did you refuse to see me or answer my calls?''

''If you had known I was pregnant, what would you have done?''

''I would have asked you to marry me.''

''Exactly.''

''You left because you didn't want to marry me,''

he stated in a cold, bleak voice. He dropped his hands and pulled away, leaving her aching for his touch.

"I left because I wanted to marry you too much."

"That's crazy." Anger filled his voice and stiffened his muscles. He jumped from the swing and strode across the porch.

"Is it?" she asked sadly. "You've never made a secret of your reluctance to marry. I've always known your feelings on the subject, just as well as I've known how honorable you are."

"Then why did you leave me?"

The anguish in his cry grieved her. "If you had discovered I was pregnant, you would have *insisted* on marrying me, despite your feelings on the subject."

"Would that have been so terrible?"

She tilted her head to look at him. "It would have been glorious. But it wouldn't have lasted. Eventually you would have grown angry and bitter because you'd been forced into marriage. I didn't want to witness the love dying in your eyes and resentment taking its place."

"I was a fool. I believed that by not marrying I could spare myself the pain I'd seen my friends go through when the ones they loved left them by death or divorce."

"And now?"

"You've opened my eyes the past few days. When you came so close to dying after Blain knifed you, I realized I'd be a fool not to spend every moment I can with you."

Elation battled with despair within her. "That's

why I have to go back to St. Petersburg with Chip and never see you again."

He jerked his head up in surprise. "What?"

"I want more than just spending time with you."

He returned to the swing and gathered her in his arms. "I'm offering more. I want you to marry me. Even if Chip had never been born, I'd be asking you. I want to marry you, Heather. And, God willing, we'll grow old together." He crooked his finger beneath her chin and riveted her with a solemn look. His expression and the seriousness of his tone told her he'd meant what he'd said. "Will you marry me?"

She placed her cheek against his heart while her own swelled with happiness. Not only would he make a wonderful husband, his love and protection of Chip had already proved him a first-class father.

"Yes," she murmured.

He grew suddenly still. "What did you say?"

She threw her head back and laughed with joy. "Absolutely, positively, most definitely *yes*."

His shout of exhilaration echoed in the night. Lifting her off her feet, he covered her lips with his.

Moments later, they broke apart as headlights swept the porch and the Wades' station wagon pulled into the drive. The rear door opened and Chip hopped out.

"Mommy!" He raced across the lawn.

Heather met him at the foot of the porch steps and swung him into her embrace. He clasped his pudgy arms fiercely around her neck.

"Hi, fella," Dylan said, standing beside her.

Chip looked at him, grinned and held out his arms. "Hi, Dyl."

Dylan swung Chip onto his shoulders. Watching her son with his father brought tears of happiness to her eyes.

"Chip, it's time you started calling Dylan Daddy."

"Hi, Daddy."

"Hello, son." Dylan's voice was hoarse and his eyes moist. One arm held Chip securely on his shoulder. The other tugged her close to his side. "Welcome home."

Epilogue

One year later

Heather leaned back in the Adirondack chair with a contented smile. It had been a wonderful six-month wedding anniversary party for her and Dylan.

Talbot and her father sat on the love seat across from her, holding a sleeping Chip between them and watching Lily, Jasmine and her mother chase a giggling year-old Jennifer across the lawn.

Learning that Heather was their daughter and Chip their grandson, along with the excitement of the birth of Jennifer, Jasmine and Rand's daughter, had helped ease the pain of Blain's death for Talbot and Lily. Charles Wilcox's death from a stroke a few months ago had closed a sordid chapter in all their lives.

When Talbot and Lily had made a special trip to Fort Lauderdale to thank the Taylors for their fine job of raising Heather, the two couples had become fast friends, eliminating any sense of rivalry or tension that might have developed.

"A penny for your thoughts," Talbot said quietly.

Heather gazed out over the waters of Dolphin Bay,

sparkling in the June sunlight. "I wish I could somehow save today to keep forever. My life's been full
of peaks and valleys, but today I've reached the sum-
mit of happiness."

"Married to a good man like Dylan," her father
said, "you can count on lots of happy days ahead."

She sought out Dylan among the group gathered
behind the house beneath the wind-gnarled oaks. He
and Rand, with good-natured, if not very helpful, su-
pervision by Sid Bullock and her brothers Art and
T.J., were marking off an area for a deck across the
back of the house.

With money from the insurance settlement on Dylan's house and the sale of her own, she and Dylan
had purchased the vintage Dutch Colonial home on
the bay and spent the past year restoring it. Several
projects awaited completion, but Chip's room was
finished, as well as the nursery. She glided her hand
across her still-flat stomach. Good things always
came to her in December. Chip's birth. Her marriage
to Dylan. And next December, the arrival of another
baby.

As if sensing her thoughts, Dylan raised his head
and gazed at her across the shaded yard. The love
shining in his eyes bolstered her contentment. In
spite of his earlier resistance to marriage, he had settled happily and comfortably into his role of husband
and father. More than that, he delighted in it.

Shortly after returning to work after the frightening
incidents of a year ago, he had received a promotion
to detective-sergeant and now worked as Sid Bullock's partner. With only a few exceptions, his new

position meant regular hours and more time to spend with his family.

He left the group discussing the merits of the deck's location, ambled across the lawn and held out his hand to her.

"Mind if I borrow my wife for a few minutes?" he asked Talbot and her father.

"Go ahead," her father said. "We'll watch Chip."

With curiosity quickening, Heather accompanied Dylan to the house, through the big, sunny kitchen and into the living room with its spacious bay windows and gleaming heart-pine floors.

She challenged him with raised eyebrows. "What's this all abou—"

His lips muffled her question, and she yielded to his embrace. When he released her minutes later, she straightened her clothes and smoothed her hair.

"If I go back outside looking like this, they'll know what we've been up to."

He broke into the grin that would always make her legs weak and patted her stomach. "If they don't know already, they will in a few months."

She returned his smile. "You're impossible."

His expression sobered. "I know. And you're an angel and a saint to love me."

She caressed the strong line of his jaw. "Loving you is the easiest and smartest thing I ever did."

He kissed the palm of her hand, then crossed to the desk beside the fireplace, opened a drawer and withdrew a small gift-wrapped package. "This is for you."

"You always said you weren't big on presents," she protested.

He sank onto the sofa and pulled her into his arms. "I wasn't big on marriage, either, but you managed to change my mind. Now, open it."

She fumbled with the ribbon and paper and opened the small box. Nestled in the velvet lining was an antique gold locket on a thin gold chain. She opened the locket to find a tri-fold frame. Two of the frames held pictures, one of Dylan, taken on their wedding day, and another of Chip from his second birthday party.

"The baby's picture will go in the third," he said.

Her eyes misted with happy tears. "It's beautiful. Will you put it on me?"

"Read the inscription first."

She closed the locket and turned it over. *All my love forever, Dylan* was engraved on the back.

She slipped her arms around his neck. "Forever is a long time."

"For loving you?" He pulled her close and his lips moved against her forehead. "Two times forever wouldn't be long enough."

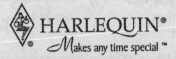